living the
dream

Look out for more missions from

MEL BEEBY
AGENT ANGEL

living the dream

ANNIE DALTON

HarperCollins *Children's Books*

Love and thanks to Terry Hong for taking time out from a busy life to advise me on aspects of Mel's twelfth and final adventure. Also a huge thank you to undercover angel Sophie Panuthos for her insights and suggestions.

First published in Great Britain by HarperCollins *Children's Books* in 2008.
HarperCollins *Children's Books* is a division of HarperCollins*Publishers* Ltd,
77-85 Fulham Palace Road, Hammersmith, London, W6 8JB.

www.harpercollinschildrensbooks.co.uk

1

Text copyright © Annie Dalton 2008

ISBN-13 978-0-00-716142-3
ISBN-10 0-00-716142-5

Mixed Sources
Product group from well-managed
forests and other controlled sources
www.fsc.org Cert no. SW-COC-1806
© 1996 Forest Stewardship Council
FSC

FSC is a non-profit international organisation established to promote the
responsible management of the world's forests. Products carrying the FSC
label are independently certified to assure consumers that they come
from forests that are managed to meet the social, economic and
ecological needs of present and future generations.

Find out more about HarperCollins and the environment at
www.harpercollins.co.uk/green

CHAPTER ONE

Trainee angels have a saying: if you want the Universe to laugh out loud, tell it your plans! Set these lyrics to a funky beat and you'd have the perfect soundtrack for my life.

I had a *ton* of stuff planned the day after my thirteenth birthday: hook up with friends in a nearby mall, check out the new pancake place, catch a movie, eat a LOT of M&Ms. *Nowhere* on this To Do list did it say: *get hit by a stolen car and turn into an angel.* Yet, on that happy sunny morning in July, somewhere between my home and Park Hall shopping centre – *BAM!* – I got an unexpected cosmic upgrade. Mel Beeby, the human schoolgirl, was history.

In the *human* world I was history. But there's so, SO

much more to this vast shimmery Universe than humans! Remember in *The Wizard of Oz*, when the dreary black and white picture suddenly explodes into Technicolor? Arriving in the Afterlife feels a bit like that, except it's not just colours, but unearthly scents, sounds, energies...

After the first shock wore off, Heaven felt deeply familiar. It felt, actually, like coming home; like, once upon a time, this luminous world of Love and Light was all we knew, then in the full-time craziness of being human we somehow forgot.

I still miss my friends and family, but these days I don't much miss being human. Going back now would feel, well, just *wrong*; like a butterfly trying to turn itself back into a caterpillar. Yet, until recently, I always had this gigantic question mark hanging over me.

WHY ME?

Out of all the hundreds of kids heading for the shopping centre that morning, what made the Angel Academy award *me* a place on their spangly new training programme? If my teachers even knew, they weren't saying. I just had to accept that I'd probably never know why the Agency wanted me on their team.

Then a v. strange sequence of events led to me solving this riddle once and for all. I finally found out why the Agency picked me for their fast-track cosmic training scheme. Better still, I found out what I'm meant to be doing from now on.

It started when I came back from my mission to India where I had to watch over a very special four-year-old boy, a future buddha, destined to be a world peacemaker. This mission was just the latest in a series of humongous, life-changing experiences. I'd just had my first cosmic upgrade, which is pretty humongous in itself. Ideally you'd need weeks of peace and quiet to adjust to all the whizzy new energies swirling round your system. I literally had like, two hours! My upgrade party was just getting into full swing when I was told I had to go back to my old school to save my human friends from the Powers of Darkness. THEN my cosmic upgrade properly kicked in, sending me totally bonkers, and I found myself going through a harrowing angelic ordeal known as The Test.

I kind of understand now why trainee angels need to go through this gruelling initiation. Being an angel in Heaven is a doddle, let's be honest! In Heaven, everything constantly reminds you that you are a luminous being of Love and Light. Unfortunately angels carry out most of their missions on Earth where, as you know, things are a *teensy* bit less loved-up.

Go to any city in my century and you'll see humans

just surviving, living as if they have no soul. This is NOT how things are supposed to be, and they didn't get this way by accident. There's a cosmic war going on – and I really hate to scare you, but the wrong side is winning.

The Powers of Darkness WANT you to think life is depressing and meaningless. They want you to feel so overwhelmed at how grim life on your planet is becoming that you have to tune it all out and just sleepwalk through your days. Sleepwalking humans are MUCH easier to control than feisty, wide-awake ones.

The Agency, the cosmic outfit I work for, beams Love and Light at your planet 24-7 to remind you who you are and what you were put on Earth to do. Meanwhile the Dark Agencies, aka the PODS, go flat out to cause chaos, destroying everything and everyone that is beautiful and good.

Sabotage, mayhem and destruction are what the Dark Agencies do best. They'll do every low thing they can think of to trip up a newbie angel and throw her off track. All those weaknesses (yes, even angels have weaknesses!), all those dark little secrets we try so hard to hide – the PODS have it ALL on file, and when the moment comes, they'll use it. The question is, when the PODS start piling on the poo, what kind of angel are you then?

That's what the Test is designed to find out. The Test,

you see, is where you finally get to meet your Dark Side face to face. Totally alone, with no cosmic support of any kind, you will be taunted and tempted by the Powers of Darkness like you would not believe.

I survived. I even came through the experience a smidge wiser than I went in. Hopefully it has made me a stronger angel. There was no time to rest on my laurels though. Only days after I got back to Heaven I had to rush off again, to twenty-first century India this time, to deliver the special little boy I told you about to some monks.

All these experiences coming so close together had left me with a LOT to think about. To pile on the stress, I'd come back to a massive backlog of school work. Every angel kid over the age of twelve has to go on missions at our school, and we're *still* expected to keep up with assignments. Considering our teachers are angels, they show no mercy whatsoever!

My punishing daily routine now went like this: shower, dress, jog down to the beach to send dawn vibes to the Universe (my new resolution), then rush off to school where I spent my day either a) in class b) in the library, catching up on coursework or c) on class field trips to deeply depressing time periods as part of Mr Allbright's ongoing module on human prejudice.

After school (assuming I wasn't too depressed by the

witch trials in seventeenth-century Salem, or whichever it happened to be that day) I'd fit in an hour at Angel Watch sending vibes to trouble spots on Planet Earth. I'd seen too much human suffering while I was in India and this was my v. puny attempt to make a difference.

OK, now that last bit is *almost* completely true. I genuinely did want to make a difference. But it's also true that I was putting off the tricky moment when I had to be all alone in my room. I couldn't exactly hang out at Angel Watch (or my fave café, or the school library) until morning, and believe me I'd tried! Sooner or later the moment always came when I had to force myself back to the school dorm to squeeze in an hour's revision for the end of term exams, and (oh, yes!) being outstared by a several billion-years-old Creation angel.

Ah, now that's the part that wasn't supposed to happen.

CHAPTER TWO

The night the angel first appeared, I'd just got back from India so it was a shock, but it was an Indian kind of shock. A visitation from a seven-foot-tall, golden-eyed angel fitted right in with all the mystical happenings of the past few weeks.

This angel hadn't been taking care of himself at *all*. His hair hung in matted locks like Indian holy men, and he gave off a truly desperate vibe, like street people I'd seen in India, as if he'd been pushed over some invisible edge and couldn't see a way back.

He said he'd come to thank me for taking care of the child buddha we'd been watching over. Then he asked me to save the world. He didn't use those actual words,

I want you to save the world, Melanie, but we both knew that's what he meant.

I said, "But I'm just a kid." He can't have thought that was a good excuse because after that he came back every night.

Just so you understand how weird this was, I should explain that Creation angels are TOTALLY not social beings. They don't mix with other types of angels – they don't even hang out *that* much with other Creation angels; they're such pure, supersensitive beings they prefer to keep in touch by telepathy as they go about their work. Humans don't seem to realise, but Creation wasn't some one-time-only special deal that happened with a big flourish of trumpets back in the day then like, *stopped*! Creation is never-ending! If you were able to see Earth through our eyes, you could spot Creation angels at work all over your planet, transforming cosmic energy into moss or flowers, watching over life forms from the teeniest little beetles to huge, chest-thumping gorillas.

Creation angels love Earth the way a mother loves her new baby or an artist loves her painting. They love it so much, it's actually physically distressing for them to leave.

A Creation angel coming back to Heaven, *attaching* himself to a lowly trainee angel, literally *demanding* her help. It was totally unthinkable!!

Admittedly, after that first night, he gave up hassling

me in any way. He was just *there*, filling my room with v. disturbed emotions: despair, fury, grief – feelings I can't even describe.

A disturbed seven-foot-tall angel staring reproachfully at the back of your neck doesn't exactly help your concentration. Plus, I know this sounds pathetic, but if I needed to change into my PJs, I felt like I should do it in the bathroom, the only place I was sure of privacy!

The worst part was when I tried to sleep. I only had to close my eyes and instantly the angel and I would be swooping through the celestial Light Fields side by side, his tawny-gold wings outstretched, like some huge, silent owl.

The flying part would have been lovely, but after that first time it felt too much like the opening moments of a recurring bad dream. Now I knew where he was taking me: back to my century, to one polluted, scorched, flooded, war-torn Earth region after another.

I'm not totally brainless. I *did* know my century was in trouble. But when someone forces you to see how humans (under the influence of the Dark Powers) are devastating your beautiful little planet, when you see how the horror just goes on and on and on, it completely blows you away.

Out of the harrowing sights the angel showed me, one still comes back to haunt my dreams. I don't really know why. It wasn't the worst thing, not by miles. We'd landed on an island, I think it was in the Pacific. White sands, palm trees, sun. It should have been paradise. Except I've seen paradise and the ocean isn't carpeted with floating bits of plastic, and the sand isn't filled with dead, or dying, sea birds. The birds had innocently tried to eat the plastic and their poor little stomachs had – sorry, there's no other word – *exploded*.

Now I get that the angel *had* to share these things with someone. He needed to make someone care as much as he cared, or maybe he just needed someone to agonise *with*? But back then I couldn't handle it. My night journeys left me so exhausted, I was having to whack on concealer to hide my dark circles. One morning I asked – actually I *begged* – Helix to help me.

Helix is my inner angel; that's like, my celestial GPS system and Jiminy Cricket all rolled into one. When I'm struggling with some knotty cosmic problem, Helix is generally v. happy to set me straight. But when I asked how I could get the Creation angel to leave me in peace, she was REALLY sharp with me!

Ever thought of TALKING to him? she snapped, as if she was talking to an extremely dense child.

I was like: "Have you ever *tried* to have a conversation with a billion-year-old Creation angel? Well, I have, so I'll tell you *exactly* how it would go.

Angel: *It is your task to save the world.* Melanie: 'No, it's not! Reason One: I've been an angel for like, FIVE minutes. Reason Two: I have NO world-saving abilities whatsoever.' Angel: *It is your task to save the world...*"

There was a pause, then Helix said crisply: *Sorry, angel girl, you're on your own with this one.*

I said something sarky, like, "Well, thanks SO much for your input, Helix!" Then I spoiled it by bursting into tears.

In the end I fell back on the strategy I used when my dad walked out and I started having bad dreams. I completely forced myself to stay awake. Instead of sleeping I sat up revising, or I texted my friend Lola who was still away on some big mission, or I played my most vibey music and drank gallons of strong hot chocolate...

Several times I fell asleep at my desk with my face *smooshed* against a pile of books. Each time the angel was waiting with new scenarios to break my heart: tiny polar bear cubs drowning because the ice had become so thin they just fell through into the freezing waters below; Amazonian rainforests being reduced to acres of stinking charcoal; dying coral reefs like bleached boneyards.

All the time the angel was beside me with his

wounded golden eyes. I always picked up the same despairing thought: *Angel child, this was not what we dreamed.*

CHAPTER THREE

One afternoon I was in the library, curled up on a big comfy sofa. Without looking I could feel awesome cosmic patterns slowly rearranging themselves above my head.

I wasn't such a big fan of libraries when I was human, but our school library is actually v. v. cool. The reading room has a ceiling which doubles as an actual planetarium. I'll be stressing over some assignment, then I just happen to glance up and catch the stars and planets doing their slow boogie, and it reminds me that even a lowly angel trainee is a tiny part of this vast shimmery dance.

This particular afternoon though I could barely even *focus* on the dancing planets. It had taken ten minutes to realise I was reading the wrong book! The book I thought I'd taken down from the shelf was Mr Allbright's recommended text on the Salem witch trials. The book I was holding in my hand was something like *The History of Human Tribes*. No help with my witches assignment whatsoever.

I could feel myself slowly sinking into the sofa. I had a quick glance round at the other library users peacefully taking notes. *Go on*, coaxed my inner sleepyhead. *Take a tiny catnap. He won't bother you here. He only ever comes when you're alone...*

A hot breeze swooshed into my corner of the reading room, bringing that scorched rubber smell you get in deserts, flicking through the pages of my book so fast it sounded like a gambler shuffling cards.

You fell asleep, I told myself, genuinely desperate to believe it. *You're asleep in the library and this is just a dream.*

Now as well as crisply flicking pages I could hear more distant sounds as if they were reaching me from another world or another time: horses snorting, burning wood snapping and crackling, and a woman chanting in a low intense voice:

House made of the dawn.

House made of evening light.
House built of pollen...

The pages gradually stopped turning, leaving my book open at two old-style sepia photographs of a Native American boy.

Happily on a trail of pollen, may I walk.
As it used to be long ago, may I walk...

The chanting voice and the boy's intense dark eyes pulled me in. It was like I *had* to read the info under those faded old pictures.

I learned that the boy's name was Tom Torlino. He'd been born into the Navajo tribe. The two pictures were taken after he'd been forcibly removed from his village with other Navajo boys and sent away to a government-run boarding school. The authorities took before and after photos because they wanted to show that Indian kids could be "civilised" if you could just get them away from the contaminating influence of their families.

In the "before" picture, Tom Torlino wore his long black hair loosely pulled back off his face. A ceremonial blanket was draped around his shoulders. Silver hoops, the size of small coffee cups, hung from his pierced ears. Around his neck were several strings of beads and also a complicated kind of collar made from beautifully carved bones; presumably that was for protection, though he didn't seem like he needed much protecting. He looked like a boy who could wrestle a wolf if need be, a child warrior.

The second picture showed Tom after three years at the white man's boarding school. His thick glossy hair had been cropped shorter than a seal's fur. He was buttoned into an old-fashioned school uniform that looked uncomfortably tight across the chest. But in both pictures his eyes were exactly the same: fierce, proud, totally untamed.

I felt like I ought not to be looking at this dignified boy. That second picture was just wrong. What they did to Tom Torlino was wrong.

This was not what we dreamed, the angel said inside my head.

I slammed the book shut. Messing with my mind in the library was just going too far. I felt a sighing, golden breath and clamped my hands over my ears. "Go away!" I hissed. "Don't breathe in my ear, don't follow me around school and *don't* swap my books around, OK?"

Or you'll do what? I asked myself. The truth is I only had myself to blame. I should have told someone when the angel first appeared. So why didn't I? I'd asked myself this same question every night and I always came up with the same reason. I didn't tell anyone because it sounded – kind of *grandiose*.

Being "grandiose", if you didn't know, is a major no-no for angels. Mr Allbright is constantly telling us there are no superstars in the angel biz; we're all just links in a divine chain, members of a team, blahdy blahdy blah.

This teamwork thing was a v. tough concept for me to grasp when I started my training. The human Melanie prided herself on being a unique individual; so unique that on my first field trip as a bona fide angel, I broke the rules, took off on my own and almost got my mind melted by the Powers of Darkness.

So the thought of telling my long-suffering teacher that out of all the angel trainees in the Universe, I had been singled out by a Creation angel to solve Earth's environmental problems made me go hot and cold all over.

I might have gone on fretting all day, but every cell in my body suddenly sparkled to attention. My buddy Reuben had appeared at the top of the stairs, a battered old flight bag slung over his shoulder, and looking slightly too warm in his cold weather clothes. I told myself I could handle this just fine. My heart was only beating ten million times faster than normal after all.

As if life wasn't complicated enough, I'd fallen in love.

Chapter Four

They say opposites attract and Reuben and I are COMPLETE opposites. He's a super-talented musician. I sing like a cartoon frog. Reubs doesn't give two hoots what he wears. I am totally style obsessed. Even our cosmic backgrounds are drastically different. I grew up on Earth in a gritty inner city estate. Reuben grew up in Heaven.

As soon as he spotted me Reubs' face lit up.

Still deafened by my own heartbeat, I pushed back my chair and went over. "Hiya!" I said, all super-casual. "When did you get back?"

Having unwound his woolly scarf, Reuben peeled off his padded cap. "Just now!" he said, beaming.

"You came here without even dropping off your stuff?"

"I was coming to find you. Amber said you practically live in the library these days. What's going on, Beeby?" he teased. "Burning the candle at both ends? That isn't like you."

I felt my cheeks going pink. "I've got a lot of catching up to do," I said quickly, which wasn't a *complete* lie. "I missed loads when we were in India."

"I've missed more! Probably not as much as Chase though!"

Chase is a major wildlife freak. Lola describes him as half angel, half beast! He heard the Agency was after volunteers to track down a rare snow leopard and her unborn cubs. As soon as we returned from India, he dragged Reubs and Brice back off to the Himalayas, which we'd just left twenty-four hours previously!

"So what's been happening while I've been away?" Reubs asked.

I'm being haunted by a billion-year-old angel.

"Nothing much," I fibbed. "We're studying this v. depressing module on human prejudice. I'm doing an assignment on witch hunters."

"So you wouldn't mind a break?"

I pretended to think. "Hmm. Sit in the library, reading about murderous witch-hating humans, or go to Guru, drink hot chocolate and hear about the cute baby snow leopards – that's a tough one!"

"How did you know about the baby leopards?" he said, amazed. "We only found them yesterday!"

"I don't know. I just—" Then I realised what he'd said. "Omigosh, you *found* them?"

Reuben patted his jacket. "Not only found them, Beeby. I've got *pics*!"

Despite, or maybe because of, his Heavenly upbringing, Reubs is fascinated by anything and everything to do with my home planet: music, people, wildlife. I sometimes think he loves Earth even more than I do!

We hurried downstairs and out into the morning. It suddenly hit me that this was actually the first time Reuben and I had gone anywhere together that wasn't strictly work related.

I used to tell everyone Reuben was just like my angel big bro. I'd be like, "It's SO cool how we can just enjoy each other's company without any of that boy/girl stuff messing things up." Classic, right? You can totally see what's coming!

One day, when we were alone together on our first ever soul-retrieval mission, Reuben let slip that he was in love with some mystery angel girl. Then he went all mysterious on me, refusing to tell me who she was, and for some reason we both got really huffy. Things got worse when he bought Millie to be his support DJ at my birthday party. Lola remarked casually that they'd been tight since they were little kids, which *really* upset me. I mean, a normal girlfriend is one thing, but a childhood sweetheart – you'll never measure up, will you?

Miraculously, India put our friendship back on track. The stress of protecting a child buddha from the forces of cosmic evil could have driven me and Reubs even further apart, but it brought us closer; though not *quite* close enough to bring up the exact nature of his relationship with his childhood sweetheart.

Now here we were sitting on opposite sides of a window table in Guru, our fave café, and neither of us could think of *one* thing to say! I'd let myself hope that our relationship was about to enter a new and very special phase, but with a painful silence whistling through my ears like wind over the prairies, this was starting to seem like wishful thinking.

"So what's been happening while I've been away?" Reubs said awkwardly, having already asked me this exact question.

"Not a lot!" I fibbed... again.

"Settled back in OK after India?"

"Yeah, totally!"

"Have you heard how Lola's getting on?"

"A bit," I said vaguely.

"She texted me a couple of times." He frowned. "She didn't give much away. I get the feeling this mission isn't a whole lot of fun."

"She could just be mad-busy?"

"She sounds sad more than busy," said Reubs.

I felt a guilty pang. Preoccupied with my own problems, I'd taken Lola's brief jokey texts at face value.

"Take a look at these little cuties!" Reuben pushed his phone across the table.

"Omigosh, they're *so* SWEET!" I cooed over each pic of the helpless little newborns. All baby animals are sweet, but snow leopard cubs are just magic.

"I bet Chase is over the moon!"

Reubs shook his head. "We're not out of the woods yet."

"Why? What's happened?"

Reubs explained that the snow leopard's lair was on a mountain which locals believed to be sacred. Now the animals were threatened with the arrival of a new railway that was going to carve right through the holy mountain.

"Ever get the feeling humans literally want to *punish* their planet?"

"No, actually, I don't." My voice sounded sharper than I meant it to.

"That came out wrong," Reubs said quickly. "In theory I do get that the Powers of Darkness have a sneaky knack of making humankind do their dirty work for them. It's just so hard to remember when you're there though, isn't it?"

"Almost impossible," I agreed. "So if it's hard for angels, who *know* there's a cosmic war going on, it's no wonder humans get confused."

I saw that Reuben's expression had become a little fixed.

"What?" I said nervously. "I've got mascara on my nose, haven't I?"

He shook his head. "You're twiddling your hair. You always do that when you're stressing."

"I'm not stressing," I fibbed, quickly sitting on my hands. "I just hate that my century is in such bad shape."

Reuben broke into a totally luminous smile. Lola calls it his Sweetpea smile. It makes him look as if he's just received a personal message from the Universe telling him everything is going to be OK.

"I'd much rather go to times like yours," he said, "where angels and humans can really pull together and make a difference, wouldn't you?" He started delving in his flight bag, eventually bringing out a minidisc. "I burned this for you the night we got back from India.

I've been carrying it all around the Himalayas. Track one is just a Bollywood remix of 'You're not Alone'."

Lola and I loved Reubs' feel-good anthem so much we instantly adopted it as our cosmic theme tune. I even have it as my ringtone!

"Reubs, that's such a cool idea!" Reubs knows I'm mad about everything Bollywood.

"The other tracks are pretty much works in progress. Don't expect too much, OK?" Reuben looked like he half wanted to snatch it back.

"You always give me such sweet presents," I said impulsively.

He looked alarmed. "Do I?"

"Yeah, you do! You gave me that bear."

Reuben gave an embarrassed laugh. "I just won that at the fair. I wasn't exactly going to keep a big blue teddy for myself!"

And you gave me that charm bracelet for my birthday, and once you brought me back a tropical flower from the Heavenly interior, just because you knew I was having a bad time. I didn't say that part aloud. Reuben looked hot and bothered as it was. I was pretty hot and bothered myself!

At that moment Mo appeared with our order. "I forgot to say congratulations, you guys," he said, beaming. We stared at him blankly.

"Congratulations for...?" I said cautiously.

"For delivering Obi safely to the monks! The little buddha?"

"Oh, *right*! Thanks!" I tried to sound polite, although I was actually longing for him to go away. Reubs patiently answered Mo's questions, describing our last glimpse of Obi as he set out on the rope bridge to the hidden monastery.

I pretended to dab up crumbs from my muffin, but I was suddenly incapable of swallowing. All the colours had drained out of the café. The angel's ominous words rang in my ears: *And when he walks back across the bridge as a young man, what kind of planet will he see?*

Eventually Mo left to serve some new customers. Reuben lightly touched my hand. "What's wrong?"

But I couldn't bring myself to tell him. I mean, it was happening to me and even *I* didn't believe it half the time. I fiddled unhappily with the minidisc case where Reubs had scrawled his playlist:

track 1, ur not alone b'wood mix
track 2 earth dreams
tracks 3, 4 & 5

I felt a smile start somewhere deep inside my heart. One of Reubs' "works in progress", that he said he'd burned the night we got back from India, was called "Melanie's Song".

THREE versions! In that moment I knew I could tell this angel boy anything and he wouldn't think I was bigging myself up; he'd just accept what I said because...

"Reubs," I said, throwing caution to the wind. A chime of bells came from his mobile.

He groaned. "Chase said he'd call if we get the green light to head back out on our snow leopard project." He left the table to take his call. When he came back, he couldn't stop grinning.

"I'm guessing it's good news! That's fantastic, Reubs," I added, injecting oodles of enthusiasm into my voice. "Congratulations." (Well, no one likes a clingy angel girl, do they?)

"Thanks!" he said shyly. "We've got a briefing at the Agency in an hour. We're leaving as soon as they find us a time slot." He pulled his chair up next to mine. "You were going to tell me something?"

A pair of hands came down over my eyes. "I'll give you a clue," said a voice. "I'm handsome and I'm dangerous!"

"That's two clues," I pointed out wearily. "Actually, until the 'handsome' bit I was going to say Brice." If there had been a painless ejector button, I'd have fired him through the ceiling into the celestial Light Fields.

Lola's boyfriend and reformed cosmic dropout dropped his hands, laughing. "Nice going," he said to Reubs, grabbing a chair. "Chase says you got the snow leopard gig." Brice dresses totally in black, which makes the bleached blond spikes in his hair even more of a contrast. Across his T-shirt was a message in teeny letters:

IF YOU CAN READ THIS YOU'RE STANDING ON MY AURA!

"We could use another team member," Reuben told him.

Brice shook his head. "Michael says I'm grounded till I hand in my overdue paper on Skin Walkers."

"What are Skin Walkers?" I asked, totally not caring.

Brice gave a pretend shudder. "You don't want to know." (Which was actually true.)

"You could bring your laptop and write your Skin Walker paper between watches," Reuben suggested.

"Nah! I was glad to help get things off the ground, but I'm not a Child of Nature like you and Chase."

He and Reubs started reminiscing about their trip. They've grown to be such big buddies, it's hard to believe that in his bad-boy days Brice once left Reuben for dead. Lola and I only just reached Reubs in time.

Evolution, our headmaster calls it. The mysterious force that drives life forms to take that impossible leap to the next level: caterpillars morphing into butterflies;

brown shiny little pips turning into apple trees; a damaged angel boy turning into the most loyal buddy you could ever wish for.

When I think back to that afternoon in Guru, I wonder why I didn't just volunteer to make up the numbers. OK, I'm not a Child of Nature either, but I *do* genuinely care about endangered species.

Was I scared of seeming uncool? Was I worried I'd look as if I was chasing after Reuben? Maybe a bit of both. But let me tell you something. This Universe is balanced on a TOTAL knife edge. We make these sudden *random* decisions, never ever dreaming what we're setting in motion. When I chose to stay behind, I was choosing a TOTALLY different direction for my future as an angel. I just didn't know it.

Brice and Reuben were cracking jokes now about some dodgy inn Brice took them to in the Himalayas where everything reeked of yak. I got up to leave. Our brief private moment was over, plus I had a hot library date with the witch hunters of Salem.

"Stay safe, angel boy," I said shyly to Reuben. "Have fun with the Skin Walkers, if fun is the right word," I told Brice.

I went back to the library and found the witches book straight off. No desert breezes, no chanting. It looked as if the angel had given up. I made notes for a couple of hours then I just had to go back to my room and listen to the songs Reubs had written for me. It sounds super-vain, but no one had ever written a song for me before. I practically ran across the campus!

For some reason my door didn't want to open. When I finally forced my way in, I found my room jam-packed with books from floor to ceiling. There was a teeny gap so I could reach my bed, also (to my relief) my bathroom.

I didn't need to read the book titles. I knew they'd have environmental scare words like HEAT, MELTING, CATASTROPHE. The angel had thoughtfully left a global-warming DVD on my bed. The cover had a v. depressing picture of smoking factories.

I squeezed over to my bed and perched tensely, trying to think. None of this was normal. Creation angels don't just up and leave Earth to harass other angels.

What's happening on Earth isn't normal though, said the small quiet voice of my inner angel. *What if things are so bad he can't actually DO his job any more?* It was the first time Helix had come online since we'd fallen out. I didn't want to admit it, but she was right.

But there were Cosmic Agencies completely dedicated to looking after Earth, agencies composed of super-brilliant angelic scientists all feverishly working on these *exact* problems. What could one ditzy angel trainee do that Heaven's scientists weren't doing already?

Did he seriously think I was going to read my way through several hundred books on the environment? Assuming I understood one *zillionth* of the contents?

Like a shiny little fish, a new idea swam into my mind. *He doesn't expect you to READ the books. He's trying to TELL you something, you moron!*

I got up to pace, but of course there was nowhere to pace so I squeezed over to the window, staring out over the Heavenly rooftops until I'd teased out the next shiny little thought.

He's saying that all these words have been written, the Agency has all the facts, humans have all the facts and NOTHING's changed. Earth is STILL dying.

I felt a tear splash on to my hand. For the first time I'd let myself glimpse the angel's agony, that the Universe could allow such terrible things to happen to his beautiful blue-green planet.

I was still clutching the global-warming DVD. Play time 93 mins. "You know what, angel girl?" I asked myself. "You can't read all these books, but would it totally KILL you to watch ONE measly DVD?"

On cue, the angel came shimmering out through the books. Like Helix he'd just been waiting for me to open my eyes. I'm such a slow learner sometimes!

The angel watched with unblinking golden eyes

as I took the DVD out of its case and slid it into my laptop. I stretched between two piles of books to pull down my blind, propped myself up on my pillows and pressed PLAY.

Chapter Five

The DVD had finished half an hour ago, but I still couldn't stop crying. The worst part, because I have a *très* vivid imagination, was the frog story (which isn't actually about frogs).

The guy who made the movie said that if you just lob a bunch of frogs into a pan of boiling water, they're going to die in shrieking agony. But if you place the frogs into cold water, then slowly heat frogs AND water at the same time, they will never even know they're being stewed.

The movie guy said that's *exactly* what's been happening to the human race. Earth's problems have been creeping up so slowly, humans are all like, "La la la!" When they actually need to jump out of that freaking pot and turn off the heat quick-smart!

I was blowing my nose for the twentieth time when I heard someone hammering on my door. "*Carita*, open up! This food is HOT!" Only one person calls me "*carita*".

I squeezed my way to the door and there was my soul-mate Lola Sanchez, clutching a sparkly takeaway bag from The Silver Lychee. Coming face to face with the wall of books, she said, without batting an eyelash, "OK, back to mine then!"

As soon as we were back in Lola's room, we hugged and screamed, then we jumped up and down, and hugged some more. Then I got my first proper look at my best friend. Reubs was right to be worried about her. Lola was trying to be her normal upbeat self, but her eyes looked totally haunted.

I didn't know what to say. I gave her another rather awkward hug. "Babe, you've been away too long!"

"Too long to live on trail mix." Lola started pulling cartons out of the bag. "That's why I stopped off at the Lychee. I went a bit mad though!" Delicious food smells were wafting around the room.

"No, you got just the right amount!" I said greedily. We arranged everything on Lola's coffee table and dived in with our freebie chopsticks.

"I ran into Reubs as I was coming out of Arrivals," Lola told me, shovelling in noodles. "So he finally told you! I was getting worried I'd have to tell you myself!"

I stared at her. "Tell me what?"

Lola looked thrown. "Oh, I thought he—"

I felt myself blushing to the tips of my ears. "There was maybe *something* he wanted to say," I confessed. "He gave me a CD, Lola. He's written me a song!"

"Oh, that's SO sweet!"

"Then Mo interrupted, and Chase called to say they got the snow leopard gig, and then Brice rocked up, you know how it is..."

"No, actually *chica*, how is it?" Lola suddenly narrowed her eyes. "You've obviously been crying. You look like you haven't slept in a year, and who exactly designated your room as the ecology section of the school library?"

That's how it is with soul-mates. While I'd been reading Lola, she'd been reading me, and I'm telling you, when Lola Sanchez gets that look in her eye, she could squeeze a secret out of pure granite.

"If I tell you, you won't think I'm – what's that thing trainees aren't supposed to be – *grandiose*?"

Lola helped herself to fried rice. "We're best friends! If you go grandiose on me, I'll pop your little bubble in a heartbeat!"

"You might not say that when I've finished," I said unhappily.

I started to describe my night-time ordeals. Lola's

expression got more and more sphinx-like. I felt my palms begin to sweat. I burbled on desperately, having *no* clue what she was thinking.

"Then today in the library he like, *forced* me into reading about American Indians for no reason!" I didn't want to disrespect a divine being, but it had to be said. "Actually, Lollie, I think he might be a teensy bit deranged."

My friend set down her chopsticks with a click. "Want me to tell you what I think is going on?" She sounded v. fierce. I nodded, gulping. "I think the Creation angels tried everything to wake humans up and take responsibility. They came out of their wild places, where you can still hear Earth's heartbeat, and they visited humans in their homes, offices, universities, science labs. They sought out tribal people, scientists, artists, feisty grannies, teenage kids with tattoos, old hippies, anyone who might, just *might*, give a damn. It worked."

My heart gave a leap. "Seriously?"

Lola quickly shook her head. "People are starting to wake up, but it isn't enough, Mel. It's too little too late. Then the angels heard about you saving your little buddha, chasing him through Time and Space, protecting him from the Dark Powers. They thought you were the mad, gutsy kind of angel girl they needed." She gave me an affectionate pat. "So your maverick angel volunteered to follow you home to Heaven. and plead with you to help. They must think you're really something," she added huskily.

"Will you PLEASE not say that!" I wailed. "What I know about the environment would fit on the back of a Post-it note!"

"What does Michael say?"

My hands drifted down from my face. "Actually—"

"You HAVE told him?"

"Not yet," I admitted.

"You told someone though?"

"I told *you*," I said in a small voice.

Lola was appalled. "I don't *believe* you, Mel Beeby. You've been sitting on this for – what – FOUR weeks now!"

"You don't know what it was like!" I burst out. "I'd just come back from a Mumbai slum. I'd said goodbye to Obi for like, *ninety-five* years. But still I thought I'd done a pretty good job, you know? And suddenly there's a deranged Creation angel in my room going, 'Thanks for saving the baby buddha, angel girl, but he might not live to BE a world peacemaker if the glaciers keep on disappearing from the Himalayas, and the world's rivers dry up and millions of humans lose their drinking water...'"

"Ha! So you DO know stuff about the environment."

Lola sounded like she'd caught me out.

"No, Lola, I don't! I watched a DVD, that's all!"

I suddenly remembered that my best friend had just returned from a super-tough mission and here I was being all *me me me*.

"I'm sorry—" I started.

"No," she said quickly. "*I'm* sorry. You're right. I can't even imagine what it was like."

"No, honestly, I was being a diva. Want that spring roll?"

"I'll split it with you! I'm catching up on my carbs!"

We ate in friendly silence, then I took a breath. "Lollie, there's a chance the angel's gone back to Earth, but just in case he hasn't, could I sleep in your room tonight?"

"You don't have to ask, you wally, but you've got to promise me you'll talk to Michael. If Creation angels are going to start leaving Earth, Michael needs to be told."

"But—" I started.

"But nothing, Melanie! You're phoning him first thing tomorrow, or I'm marching you back to your room and locking you *in* with the deranged angel."

"*Jeez*, I promise!" But I was laughing. I felt better than I had in ages.

While Lola had a shower, I fetched my duvet and made up a cosy nest with her cushions. We got under our quilts and Lola turned out the light.

"How was your mission anyway?" I remembered. "You never said where you went." When she didn't answer, I raised myself on one elbow. "Lola?"

All I heard was breathing. My exhausted friend had fallen asleep in fifty seconds flat.

CHAPTER SIX

I was in Michael's office (not the swanky suite of offices he uses down at the Agency, but his little cubbyhole office at school) waiting for him to come out of a meeting.

His assistant Sam had wangled me an appointment. As archangel with special responsibility for humankind, Michael is constantly being called to human trouble spots. Every time I see him he's either just leaving for Earth or he's just come back. Yet despite his hectic cosmic schedule, he somehow always manages to be there when we really need him.

A *whoosh* of energy parted my hair as Michael walked in. He has *the* most beautiful eyes. Beautiful, scary, totally all-seeing.

"I was wondering when you'd come," he said, smiling. My heart sank into my boots. Michael had known about the angel ALL the time.

Of course he knew, you birdbrain, I scolded myself. *He's an all-seeing, all-knowing being.* In one part of my mind I know this perfectly well, yet I still try to keep these lame little secrets. I started stammering out excuses. "I just – I couldn't understand why he chose me – I suppose I thought it was another mistake."

Michael looked puzzled. "*Another* mistake?"

Like being made an angel. It had taken me two terms to grasp that my surprise fast-track scholarship wasn't down to some embarrassing cosmic computer error.

"I just thought it had to be a mistake," I repeated pathetically. The longer Michael looked at me the more I squirmed.

"Ambriel," he said. I had no idea what "ambriel" meant. It sounded like a dessert.

Michael smiled. "The Creation angel who came to you for help. His name is Ambriel." I'm ashamed to say it had never once occurred to me to ask the angel's name.

"When you were helping at the nursery, did you ever hear Miss Dove telling the children the story of Creation?" Michael asked. I've got used to Michael's apparently random changes of subject. I shook my head, waiting for him to explain.

"She tells them how a star exploded, and the Creation angels took some of the molten star material and made a new planet. They took more star stuff and dreamed it into oceans, forests, mountains and deserts. When the planet was up and running, seas teeming with fish, trees heavy with fruit, beehives full of honey, they used the remaining star material to make humans. For thousands of years, humans lived contentedly. When disputes broke out, they always remembered that all Earth's life forms were connected. They had all come from inside the same star."

"That must have been a long time ago," I said huskily. Miss Dove's Creation story had left me with a funny little ache in my chest.

Michael nodded. "You're right. Humans gradually forgot who they were and why they came to live on Earth. But we expected that, Melanie. It's part of the journey of human evolution. The question is, what happens now?"

"Humans DO get it together though?" I asked anxiously. "Lola's from the twenty-second century so the human race can't like, totally go up in *flames*?"

"That's a tricky one!" Michael sighed. "It depends on humans in your century waking up. It depends if they're ready to live the dream."

"Michael, sorry to butt in." Sam, Michael's assistant, had come in without me noticing. "We've really got to decide what to do about Cody Fortuna."

I've been an angel long enough to realise that I'm just one tiny piece of pepperoni on the cosmic pizza. Stars are born, stars die, centuries come and go, but a human in trouble has top priority.

"I should go. There's loads of stuff I should be doing," I said quickly.

To my surprise Michael asked me to stay. "If you can spare the time?"

Each time I replay that moment I get the shivers. You seem to be heading merrily in one direction, then at the last minute – whoosh! – you make some random little decision that alters the entire direction of your life. I might not have stepped out on to that pedestrian crossing, I might not have stayed to hear Cody Fortuna's story, then I never would have found out how I'm supposed to help save the world.

CHAPTER SEVEN

The screen on Michael's laptop filled with falling leaves, spinning down from the trees and lying on the towpath of a canal. Some floated on the surface of the water looking like layers of colour in an oil painting. The location typed itself neatly across the screen: **Potomac, Montgomery County, Maryland, USA.**

The Agency camera showed a dark-haired girl in a padded jacket tugged along the towpath by six pedigree dogs. Three were so dinky you could have hung them off your car mirror. One was a giant labradoodle that looked like it had got a curly perm. Two were gorgeous huskies.

"Cody set up her own dog-walking business a few

months ago," Sam explained. "The family was struggling to pay her mum's medical bills."

I leaned forward to get a better look. Cody had jet black hair, pale brown skin and that bland expression teenagers adopt to hide their worries. We saw her returning the dogs to houses that looked like millionaires' mansions, then jogging back through the super-smart part of Potomac village.

Cody's home was in an annex attached to another of Potomac's super-size millionaire pads. The tiny cottage was painted pale primrose yellow with slate-grey shutters. One of those cool American postboxes you see in movies was nailed to the gate. Inside the cottage everything was crazily mismatched. I thought the vibey colours and vintage patterns were fun and funky.

Cody herself was not a vibey colour girl. After she changed out of her dog-walking clothes, everything she put on was in a different shade of grey. (Who knew there were so many!) I absolutely loved her style though: short tops layered over longer tops, a short skirt over leggings, thick socks under big basketball boots which Cody, or somebody, had hand-painted with teeny skulls. I wasn't sure the skulls were a healthy sign.

Cody went to find her mum who was in her dressing gown looking out at the falling leaves, sipping her morning coffee.

"Remember you need to eat some food before you take your tablets," Cody said anxiously. "You *do* know black coffee doesn't count? Has Elliot left already? The car's gone."

"Elliot's her mum's boyfriend," Sam explained. "He's Mr Billmeier's chauffeur and general dogsbody."

Cody grabbed a bagel from the bread bin, slathered on cream cheese and pointedly gave half to her mum.

"Who's talking about breakfast!" her mum joked. "You can't survive at school on half a bagel either." Her smile was bright, but kind of shaky. You could feel the effort it was taking for her to behave like a normal mum.

"No time for breakfast," Cody said. "I got two detentions for being late this month already." She kissed her mum's cheek. "See you later. And EAT, or there'll be BIG trouble!"

We sped through Agency film footage showing Cody at her high school, where she seemed like a totally different person – shy, aloof, set apart from the giggly teenage girls in their pastel sweaters. Cody did have one friend called Sheridan. She wore a studded belt through her skin-tight jeans, printed with the word MISFITS. Her dyed red hair fell over her eyes in that moody emo style and her sooty-black eye make-up made her look just a *teensy* bit like the Undead. Their friendship seemed a bit one-way to me, with Cody listening to Sheridan's endless boyfriend troubles.

We fast-forwarded to Cody's birthday, when she and her mum went hiking on a local nature trail. Later Cody bought them lunch at The Old Angler's Inn. They sat out on the deck where it was sunny. Her mum sparkled desperately all through the meal. It was painful to watch.

She isn't well, I thought. *That's why she can't pay for lunch. That's why Cody works as a dog walker to pay the bills.*

Later Cody and her mum curled up by a cosy wood fire in their cottage, watching a movie. Then Elliot, the boyfriend, came back, wanting to watch the Washington Redskins play so Cody's mum quickly switched channels.

Because it was her birthday Elliot had brought Cody a tub of her fave Ben & Jerry's ice cream. On balance though, I preferred Elliot's dog, a young labrador called Buddy, to Elliot.

"Hey, Julia," Elliot said with his mouth full. "Got a job opportunity for you. The help quit up at the house, and the Billmeiers have a big party coming up. I told Mr Billmeier you'd help out."

Julia flushed all the way down to her neck. "Oh, I don't—"

"It's just house cleaning, Jools," he said impatiently. "Absolutely no stress involved and we need the cash.

You don't seem to realise, but those doctors' bills don't pay themselves."

Julia's eyes went very bright. "Of course I know that. I – I'll go see the Billmeiers tomorrow."

"Mum," said Cody. "You don't have to—"

"No, Elliot's right!" Cody's mum was sitting bolt upright like she was about to take an exam. "It's a job opportunity, like Elliot says, and I'll make the most of it. I keep our house nice, don't I? I'll keep the Billmeiers' house nice too, *no problemo*!"

Elliot gave her a sudden dark look. "Don't go letting me down now, Jools, OK?"

Michael paused the film, explaining what I'd half guessed. Cody's mum had been in and out of hospital most of Cody's life. Julia was what doctors call "bipolar": This meant she had extreme, totally uncontrollable mood swings. Julia's "highs" were super-fun, at least to start with. Every meal was a feast, every day was a party, until the party vibe got too wild and Julia spun out of control, crashing down into depression. In her depressed state, she often couldn't take care of herself, let alone look after Cody. Then she'd be put on some new medication or whatever and for a while she'd be OK.

Once she took on the cleaning job for the Billmeiers, Julia grew increasingly fragile. We watched clips of a tense Thanksgiving. Cody's mum tried to cook a huge turkey with the traditional pumpkin pie, sweet potatoes and whatever, but only ended up burning herself and bursting into floods of tears. You'd think Elliot could have helped, but he just stormed out.

Cody smoothed antiseptic cream on Julia's burns, put her to bed still sobbing, then went to stack the dishwasher. She spent the rest of Thanksgiving watching TV all by herself, except for Buddy the labrador who rested his head on her lap with an adoring expression.

Suddenly her mum appeared, protecting her head in her arms as if she was dodging flying missiles. "Baby, could you put your hands on my head?" she begged. "It always helps when you put your hands on my head."

"I'm coming, Mom," Cody said quickly. "Go back to bed and I'll be right there."

Julia hung on to her sanity by a thread until the first week of spring when she had a total collapse and was admitted to hospital. Elliot wasn't willing to take responsibility for Cody, so she was taken into care.

In the next clip Cody was perched on a bolted-down plastic chair in an institutional-type waiting room, looking like the survivor of a bomb-blast, absolutely shell-shocked. A tired-looking woman was with her, presumably her social worker.

Cody kept saying, "When can I see my mom? Can I at least call her?"

Michael paused the movie on Cody's frozen face.

"Don't they have friends or relatives who can take her in?" I asked, dismayed. But Julia had cut herself off from her family, and her friends had too many problems of their own to take on a teenage girl.

"Cody has a guardian angel though?"

"At this present moment, no," Michael admitted. "In fact finding a guardian angel for Cody is proving to be something of a challenge." I was shocked to the core when they told me Cody had worked her way through FIVE guardian angels.

"We're looking for a permanent GA obviously," said Sam. "But Cody has quite special cosmic needs."

"She does?" I said, surprised.

Michael's assistant sailed on without actually explaining. "So it's even more vital we get the right match or we could end up doing more harm than good. We've got Cody on twenty-four hour Angel Watch, but what she needs is one-to-one cosmic support."

I looked back at the pinched, wide-eyed face on the screen. Humans react to stress in different ways. Some fight, some take flight; other people, like Cody Fortuna, retreat deep inside themselves, trying to protect what little they have left.

"I'll do it." The words jumped out of my mouth. I wasn't even sure it was me who said it. I had that tiny hot potato sensation in the centre of my chest I get when Helix is online.

Michael frowned. "Before you race to sign up there's something you should know." He gave Sam a glance I couldn't read.

"Cody Fortuna thinks she's under a curse," Sam said.

Lola came running up to me as I hurried out into the sunshine. "How'd it go?"

I beamed at her. "Good! I'm leaving tomorrow!"

Lola was gobsmacked. "You're leaving to save the *world*?"

We stared at each other, confused. A lot can happen to an angel in an hour. Completely distracted by Cody's troubles, I'd forgotten why I'd gone to see Michael in the first place!

"I'm such a birdbrain!" I wailed. "I got totally side-tracked! Sam and Michael were concerned about an American girl who's been taken into care. It turned out the poor kid didn't even have a guardian angel. I said I'd be a stand-in until they get her a permanent GA. I forgot all about saving the planet." I felt SO stupid. I mean how can you *forget* an entire planet?

Instead of yelling, Lola looked intrigued. "Sounds like you didn't have a choice. This girl's obviously overdue some cosmic support."

"She hasn't got any other kind going, that's for sure," I sighed. "Have you got a minute, Lollie?"

Lola checked her watch. "I'll give you ten," she said with a slight smirk, "then I have a study date in the library with Brice."

We found a sunny spot on the library steps. Michael and Sam had filled me in on a few more biographical details before I left so I shared some of Cody's unusually troubled life with Lola.

Cody's dad, Martin Fortuna, was part Navajo Indian. For the first two years of Cody's life the three of them lived in Tucson, Arizona, a few miles from the Navajo reservation where Martin grew up. Julia met Cody's dad when he walked into the tiny art gallery where she worked. It was love at first sight. Julia told her friends that Martin was her lucky charm. She felt so safe with him, she said she knew she'd never have another bad spell as long as she lived.

In the early days of their marriage Martin often drove Cody and her mum out to the reservation to hang out with his relatives. But when Cody was two and a half, something triggered one of Julia's bad spells. When Julia got ill, she often thought people were plotting against her. Someone would say something she didn't quite catch, nothing to do with Julia at all, but her mind would seize on it as proof that her worst fears were true. Somehow she got it into her head that her Navajo in-laws were jealous of her and actually wanted to harm her and her child. She was so terrified she immediately made plans to leave for Washington DC, hundreds of miles away.

Martin found out and the couple had an ugly fight. Julia screamed at her husband that his "retarded relatives" would never see their child again. A distraught Martin yelled at her in Navajo as his wife and little daughter drove away for ever. From then on, each time they got thrown out of their lodgings, or the car got a flat tyre, or she lost another job, Julia said it was because Cody's father had cursed them. In the past three years Cody and her mum had moved house EIGHT times.

"If it was an actual bona fide curse, it's too late for Martin to take it back. He died in a car smash a few weeks later." I took a breath. "Am I mad, Lollie? For taking her on, I mean? This kid's burned her way through five guardian angels. Maybe she really *is* under a curse?"

"Remember when we did curses in Dark Studies?" Lola asked. "The teacher said when someone's under a curse, it's like they're trapped in a circle of darkness they can't step out of, however hard they try."

I gasped. "That is SO totally Cody! Except her circle is like, pure *grey*. Seriously, Lola, she has an entire wardrobe full of grey clothes."

"Which makes you the perfect guardian angel for Cody!" For the first time since she returned from her mission, Lola's eyes had their old sassy sparkle.

"It does?" I said doubtfully.

"It TOTALLY does! You're everything Cody has forgotten how to be. Positive, sparkly, vibey..."

I threw my arms around her. "Lollie, thank you!"

"What did I do?"

"Everything!"

It was true. Thanks to Lola, I suddenly knew what I had to do. I had to be the *angel* version of Cody: what Cody could be, what she hopefully *would* be, when her grey world finally exploded into fabulous Technicolor.

I was due to leave first thing tomorrow. That meant I only had a few hours to put my plan into action. "Gotta go!" I told Lola urgently. "I need a pair of hand-painted basketball boots for my mission."

Lola gave a surprised laugh. "Any special design?"

"Whatever's the opposite of skulls," I told her.

CHAPTER EIGHT

When I walked back into my room, loaded with carrier bags, I gave a huge sigh of relief. It was just my normal room. No wall-to-wall books, and not a trace of Ambriel.

I started unwrapping my purchases, deciding which to pack in my flight bag and which ones to wear the next day. I hadn't been shopping, not proper shopping, for aeons and I'd bought a teensy bit more than basketball boots.

Nine times out of ten, angels go absolutely unnoticed by humans. A good celestial agent shouldn't draw attention to herself. She definitely shouldn't do anything obviously angelly. (For instance, appearing to a scared little child and announcing: "For lo, I am the angel Melanie!" to use a v. embarrassing example from my first mission.) Our job is simply to help humans wake up and remember why they're on Earth. We're just like the cosmic catalyst or whatever.

However, that's no excuse to just flit about in trackie bottoms, right? Clothes matter to me and I could tell they mattered to Cody. I was going to copy Cody's quirky, layered style, but instead of all the grungy grey, my layers were shimmery earth colours.

I was pleased with my look, but I was proudest of my basketball boots, hand-painted with teeny birds and butterflies, as totally opposite from skulls as you can get.

Lola came by as I was folding a jewel-green top in tissue. She gave me an approving once-over. "I'm loving the boots, carita! Is this how Cody dresses?"

"Her style, not her colours. This girl is *deep*, Lollie. Sam says she has special cosmic needs – whatever that means," I added doubtfully.

"She's got to be quite special if she's got through five guardian angels! Anyone would think she's trying for a record. Wish I was coming with you," she added with a sigh. "I'd rather help with Cody than be stuck in the library watching grisly tapes of human prejudice field trips. Who knew the angel biz could get so – you know, *dark*." That new haunted look came and went so quickly from her face, I wasn't sure if it was just my imagination.

"You still haven't told me what happened on your trip," I said, suddenly feeling v. guilty that I hadn't tried harder to find out.

Her face clouded. "I know. I wanted to. I wanted to tell you ever since I got back. I just—"

Lola wandered over to my window. I hadn't bothered to pull down the blind and I could see city lights winking and twinkling behind her. I went to join her and realised she was trying not to cry.

"Lollie, isn't there anything I can do?" I was nearly crying in sympathy even though I had no clue what was wrong.

I don't think she heard me. She seemed to be looking through the divine shimmer of the Heavenly City into something unbelievably dark.

"Would it help to talk about it?" I started, but she softly interrupted me.

"Know why I got so mad with you about Ambriel? It's because of where I've been. Because of what I've seen."

She reached into her pocket and took out a shimmery cosmic memory stick, half the size of her little finger. "I'll show you. If you think you're up to it?" she added anxiously.

"No, I want to see." I'd lived in a Mumbai slum; I thought I was unshockable. I fetched my laptop and we sat down together on my rug. Lola plugged in the memory stick. The screen went foggy, and my tiny room filled with sounds of dripping water. I adjusted the brightness gizmo, but it still took a while to make out the anxious faces in the gloom.

"That's where I've been living," Lola said quietly. "Nine little kids and three adults living in this like, leaky hut on stilts." Lola's camera panned across a vast shanty town on stilts, built over dirty, stagnant water. Rain was pouring down out of a sky the colour of lead. There are places on Planet Earth that look disturbingly like one of the Hell dimensions.

"I was there in the rainy season," she said. "People's blankets, clothes, everything are constantly wringing wet. You smell drains and sewage all the time."

Lola explained that this family's world hadn't always been this way. "But all the fertile land where people used to grow their crops is now regularly flooded with salty water, so even when the floods die down, nothing can grow."

I thought I'd seen all the global-warming nightmares. This was one Ambriel had missed. We watched footage of little children swimming around like fish in the polluted water. You could hear their chirpy little voices laughing and teasing, sounding like kids sound everywhere.

"Don't they get sick from going in the water?"

Lola nodded. "All the time. Most kids never reach the age of four."

I stared at her in horror. "You mean they DIE?"

"The families are so poor, they can't afford to take their children to a doctor."

A police cruiser zipped by, churning up water. The younger children had to cling to the struts not to be swept away. Grim-faced cops scanned the floating slum through binoculars.

"The kids don't get any education and there are almost no jobs," Lola went on bleakly. "Pretty much the only way to make money is by selling drugs." She paused the picture on a skinny laughing boy. He was pretending to be a sea monster chasing the younger kids, making them giggle and shriek.

"That's Miguel, the boy I was sent to watch over. While I was there he got caught up in a gang war. There was nothing I could do. He died, Mel. He was eleven years old."

Lola leaned wearily against my shoulder and I knew her sadness was too deep for tears. I didn't try to comfort her. What could I say? Scientists in my century are constantly warning governments that Planet Earth is in for a hellish future if they refuse to take action. But for far too many vulnerable humans that future is here and now. For families like Miguel's, like families I saw in the slums of Mumbai, time has already run out. That's why Ambriel followed me back to Heaven in a last-ditch attempt to turn the tide.

Now, instead of helping him, I'd committed myself to getting just *one* human soul back on track. My decision didn't make a lot of sense, with the world going up in flames, but I knew I had to help Cody Fortuna. From the moment I saw her being pulled along the towpath by six panting dogs, I knew.

"I wish I could meet Cody," Lola said softly, reading my mind.

I perked up. "You can! Well, kind of. Michael gave me her Agency co-ordinates, so I can send vibes before I leave. You could help!" I said hopefully.

Lola managed a smile. "Let's do it!"

The truth is, unless we're total burned-out wrecks, angels actually feel *heaps* better doing angel work!

I double-clicked on Cody's divine computer link. The screen brightened and a new location flashed up: **Bethesda, Maryland, USA**. The care authorities must have moved her.

Cody and the tired social worker I'd seen earlier were waiting in yet another shabby outer office. A clock said 7:15. Outside it was pitch dark, but people were still tapping wearily at computer keyboards and making calls. Cody had stopped asking if she could see her mum. Her eyes were so bleak I longed to give her a hug.

A woman came out to see them. "Ms Lee?" she said sharply, though they were the only people waiting.

"I'm Celia Lee and this is Cody Fortuna," said the social worker. "We talked earlier on the phone."

The woman totally ignored Cody, talking over her head. "You're very lucky," she snapped, as if Ms Lee didn't deserve luck. "Mrs LaPlante says she'll take her. Her son is driving her over."

"Can't Mrs LaPlante drive?" asked Ms Lee, surprised.

"She's older than our usual foster mothers," the woman admitted. "A little set in her ways. Driving makes her nervous. Does the kid own a dress? Mrs LaPlante doesn't like her girls to wear jeans or sneakers."

"I never saw her in a dress," Ms Lee admitted.

"Could someone just *talk* to the *child*!" Lola yelled at my laptop.

"All that long hair will have to go," the woman added, sounding pleased for the first time. "Mrs LaPlante has this thing about..." she dropped her voice, "*infestation.*"

A light started flashing in the corner of my screen. "What's happening?" Lola asked in alarm.

"Don't ask me," I wailed. "I never did this before."

Lola peered at my laptop. "There's another camera we're supposed to be using. Click up here."

A second camera showed a couple hurrying into the building and handing in their ID to the security guy. I heard Lola suck in her breath. It wasn't just that Mrs LaPlante was old and puffy-faced and had a hairstyle that looked like it had been glued on to her head in the 1950s, or even that her son wore those icky white towelling socks with carefully ironed jeans. It was their eyes. When people get that close to the Dark Powers, there is just pure emptiness looking back at you.

"No, *no*! This mustn't happen!" Lola was tugging at her hair.

Jamming on my headset I was already on it. "Sweetie, you're in danger! Do anything it takes to buy yourself some time, but you must NOT go with these people!"

I'd been in some cosmic situations, but this was the first time I'd tried to outwit the PODS from my bedroom! Lola and I beamed the same urgent message over and over. *Do NOT go with the LaPlantes. Save yourself NOW! Do NOT go with...*"

"Ms Lee," Cody said abruptly. "My stomach feels weird again. I need to go to the bathroom."

"Oh, good GIRL!" exclaimed Lola. Cody bolted into the ladies' room.

"Cody has a nervous stomach," Celia Lee said

in an undertone. "Her file says she also suffers from night terrors."

The woman's mouth tightened like a purse. "A half-breed Indian kid with so many problems. Mrs LaPlante is going to have her work cut out."

Half-breed? Hello! I thought. *Is she a child or a dog?*

Lola was clicking on different cameras. Suddenly we were back with Cody. She was staring at herself in the mirror as if she had no idea what she was doing here.

"We can't help you out with this one, babe," I told her. "You're going to have to come up with something on your own, and it's got to be drastic, OK?"

I could see Cody thinking frantically. Suddenly she reached into her bag and took out a pair of vicious-looking nail scissors.

We both yelled, "CODY, NO!"

Cody didn't try to harm herself, but what she did was nearly as shocking. She lifted handfuls of her long, blue-black hair and started hacking off random chunks.

Lola let out a shriek. "Oh, now *that's* drastic!"

Cody worked super-fast. You could just hear tiny snipping sounds and the panicky sound of her breathing. She didn't glance in the mirror once, doing it all by feel, like she didn't even care what the end result looked like. When she'd finished, I wanted to cry.

She looked like a bird, a frightened fledgeling bird that just fell out of its nest.

Still avoiding her reflection, she was about to leave when I saw a flash of something in her eyes. She swiftly gathered up the mass of fallen hair then stuffed it down the toilet, flushing several times.

It's what you do in some cultures if you think something evil is after you. Something with your energy in it – hair, nail clippings – could give them power over you. But Cody hadn't grown up in that kind of culture. It was like some deep part of her, her Navajo DNA or whatever, had flagged up a warning.

Lola clicked back on the first camera. We saw the women's astonished faces as Cody emerged from the bathroom minus her hair. Ms Lee actually gasped. "What were you *thinking*?"

Cody's expression was carefully blank like always, but you could see she was trying not to cry. "I cut it short for Mrs LaPlante," she said in a trembling voice.

"There's short, young lady, and there's looking like you've been savaged by killer rats," snapped the child-care woman. "I'm telling you right now that Mrs LaPlante will not take on any kid who looks as – as *bizarre* – as you do now."

*Yess! **Thank you**, Universe!*

Cody's cosmic cheerleaders jumped up and down,

clapping and whooping. "Man, we are SO hot," said Lola gleefully. Then she said excitedly, "Mel, check out Celia! The angel vibes got her too!"

Ms Lee was watching Cody with a totally new expression. Until now I think she'd been trying to keep her heart closed to Cody, treating her as just one more case, but in that moment she stopped being Cody's social worker and became a real human being.

"You know what?" she said abruptly. "I haven't eaten since breakfast. I need food. How about you?"

Cody looked wary. Like, *Why's she acting so friendly?*

"I don't just mean *any* food." Ms Lee said, smiling. "I'm talking about TASTEES. It's one of Bethesda's institutions, the original greasy diner. They do *the* most fabulous fried chicken sandwiches," she told Cody. "And downright *evil* chocolate pancakes. Shall we give it a shot?"

Cody's hand crept up to her mutilated hair. Ms Lee laughed. "No one will give you a second glance at TASTEES. We'll fill up on bad carbs, then you can stay the night at my place. You'll have to sleep on the sofa, and my dogs will insist on sharing it with you."

"I like dogs," Cody half whispered.

"So let's go!" said Ms Lee. "And tomorrow, cross my

heart, Cody, I'll pull out all the stops for you. I'm not taking any crap from *anybody*, I swear!"

The child-care lady was fuming. "This is highly irregular!"

"Yes, it is," said Ms Lee sweetly. "Feel free to file a report." Cody and Celia walked out through the swing doors, past the sitting area where the LaPlantes were waiting.

"Change of plan," Celia Lee called cheerily. "So sorry you had to be inconvenienced, sir, madam!"

Back in my bedroom, my knees totally turned to water.

"That was a bit too close for comfort," I told Lola shakily. "The PODS produced those creeps *fast*. It's like they've just been waiting till she hit rock bottom."

"Eight homes in three years. Five guardian angels. Mum in and out of psychiatric hospital. Dad dead in a car smash. I'd say they've been doing more than *waiting*," said Lola fiercely. "Sounds like they've been out to *make* her hit rock bottom from day one."

"But WHY? Why target Cody?"

"All I know is she didn't come to their attention for no reason. If she has 'special cosmic needs', or whatever Sam said, you can bet the PODS know about it." Lola stood up and swayed on her feet.

"Bed," I told her sternly. I pushed her towards the

door, but she suddenly swung to face me. For an instant it was like someone else was looking out through my best friend's eyes. Someone calm and old and scarily wise.

"You think Cody's a safe Mel Beeby type mission, don't you?" she demanded. "But saving the world, that's too big to handle."

When someone sees you more clearly than you see yourself, it's *très* disturbing. "How did you know I thought that?" I said uncomfortably. I hadn't known it myself till Lola said it out loud!

"I get more psychic, remember, the tireder I get! And I'm telling you that's not how it is." Lola closed her eyes like she was channelling info from far far away. "They're not separate missions, OK? It's like – Cody is the key for you, and *you're* the key for Ambriel."

"That makes sense," I said straight-faced.

She giggled and she was totally my Lola again. "You're right! I'm way too tired to be trying to have a conversation." She gave me a hug. "Take care of yourself, *carita*."

"Keep your phone switched on," I warned her. "I'm going to need LOTS of advice, so you'd better be on twenty-four-hour standby."

I closed the door and suddenly I was like: *phone!* I'd been so focused on my new mission I hadn't thought to check my messages. A ridiculous *whoosh!* of joy went through me as I saw Reuben had left me a text.

hi angel girl, hope u liked my tunes? 2 bad we had 2 cut things short, shd hav told u face 2 face but millie is NOT my gf, so I mite hav a question 4 u when I get back

When I'd finished my packing, I put on my PJs, but instead of going to bed I sat in the rosy glow of the cute handbag lamp Lola bought me for my birthday, reading Reuben's text over and over: millie is not my gf millie is not my gf millie is not

My head was full of my planet's tragedies, yet I couldn't seem to hold them all in my head and be happy at the same time. It sounds selfish, but for that one night I wanted to be happy.

I slotted Reuben's CD into my player, found the first version of "Melanie's Song" and settled back on my pillows. I closed my eyes as Reuben's quiet, husky voice filled my room. I was still smiling to myself when the phone rang.

CHAPTER NINE

When I heard those words – *missing in action* – everything went black inside my head: no thoughts, no feelings. I threw my coat over my PJs and ran out into the night.

I kept running, across the campus, out through the mother-of-pearl gates into the streets of the Heavenly City and I didn't stop until I ran right in through the revolving doors of the Agency Tower.

The guy on the desk waved me into a free lift. It was only then, with floors flashing past, that I began to shake.

Now, surrounded by concerned faces, my mind still refused to take it in. I tried to understand how an all-powerful, all-knowing Cosmic Agency could LOSE one of its angels?

Sam said that that part of the world was known for its violent supernatural storms. One hit on Reuben's watch, raging for hours, sending tonnes of snow and rock roaring down the mountain slopes, burying houses down in the valley, killing humans and animals, blocking mountain roads. When it died down, Reubs, the mother leopard and her tiny cubs had all vanished. Nobody needed to spell out who was behind it.

"We're getting a search party together," Sam told me.

"Put my name down." It was a no-brainer. Reubs had toughened up since his first field trip to Earth, ancient Roman prisons, the slums of Mumbai, he'd seen them all and survived, but I needed to be there helping him.

"You can't go, Boo. Not now." Lola had rushed in with Brice just in time to hear.

"He'd come if it was one of us," I said fiercely.

"Not if he was committed to saving a human. Not if he'd seen what we saw last night."

Brice put his arm round me. "It's OK, angel girl, I'll go for you."

"But your assignment—"

"Stuff the assignment," he said grimly. "The Skin Walkers will wait."

When Brice first came back to school, his clothes still smelled of Hell fumes. Now he was offering to be my stand-in. My eyes slowly filled with tears.

"I'm coming too," said Lola.

"Lola, you can hardly stand *up*!"

"I'll sleep on the flight," she insisted. "I'll be fine."

"Seems like Reuben's got some good friends," Sam told me.

"We're a team. We're the Cosmic Musketeers, isn't that right, Mel?" Lola patted my cheek.

It's what we used to tell each other when we first became friends; Lola, Reubs and I were going to be the three Cosmic Musketeers zooming through Space and Time saving humans from the Powers of Darkness. I just never imagined it would be Reuben who needed saving.

Sam immediately started making calls, putting together a rescue team.

"GO!" Lola commanded, seeing me hover. "Get some sleep. I'll call as soon as there's any news."

When I finally lay down in my room in the dark, tiny electric-type tremors were still running through me. I think it was shock.

There was a sighing, golden breath. With the worst

possible cosmic timing, Ambriel was back. I was too upset even to be mad. The angel silently pressed his thumb to my forehead and we were suddenly standing on misty green grasslands, which seemed to stretch on for ever.

There were other angels, tall luminous beings, going about some task that involved not singing exactly, but hair-raisingly lovely sounds. Some stood like motionless light beams in the mist. Like lightning conductors they were drawing raw cosmic energy down to this new planet. I could feel them weaving Heavenly and Earthly energies together, anchoring them deep inside the Earth's core. It seemed like we'd arrived at a key moment in my planet's evolution. The cosmic music was building to such a fever pitch I could literally feel it fizzing through the soles of my feet.

Then it happened. In a spreading, unstoppable tide of shimmering colour and scent, the prehistoric meadow bloomed with millions and millions of flowers. I stopped breathing. It was the most amazing thing I'd ever seen.

For the first time I saw the Creation angel's stern face soften. *THIS was what we dreamed, angel girl.*

My alarm beeped me awake. Stumbling around my room like a drunk, I started getting ready for my mission. Cody Fortuna, a girl almost as messed up as her century, needed a guardian angel.

CHAPTER TEN

You know when you feel really, REALLY lonely? You know how it seems like everyone but you is in a loved-up couple or a chatty little group? That's how I felt that morning in Departures.

Queuing for my angel tags I got stuck behind three newbie trainees going on their first school field trip to Earth. Their glowing, excited faces made me feel about a million years old. A group of celestial agents wearing First World War army uniforms were cracking jokes with their colleagues. You'd never think they were setting off to one of the most hellish battlefields in Earth's history.

At last Al, my fave maintenance guy, gave me a wave. "We're ready for you, doll," he called.

I felt a rush of panic. *I wish I wasn't going off to Earth all by myself.* I slung my bag over my shoulder and started walking briskly towards the huge bay where the time capsules were waiting. Suddenly I heard someone calling my name. I was astonished to see Michael hurrying towards me.

His rumpled silver-grey suit looked like he'd slept in it as usual, and as usual, his beautiful archangel eyes were full of the recent human troubles he'd seen, but the concern in his smile made hot tears fill my eyes.

"I wanted to wish you luck," he said quietly, "and to thank you for agreeing to be Cody Fortuna's GA. This morning you must be wondering if you made the right decision. I just want you to know that this mission – well, it's bigger than you know." He briefly touched my hair. The inside of my head turned deep sparkling blue as the jolt of archangel energy sizzled down my spine. There must have been a billion other places Michael urgently needed to be, but he waited, calmly smiling, until the door to the fragile-looking capsule slid shut and I was blasted out of Heaven.

In my shimmery glass pod, hurtling through the Light Fields, I composed endless texts to Reuben. I told him to stay strong, that we'd find him no matter where the PODS had taken him. Typing words on to the tiny screen, making myself believe he'd get to read them, felt like the only thing that stopped me going mad with worry.

The time pod dropped me outside a large white-painted house on the outskirts of Bethesda. Someone had planted dwarf daffodils in pots. A chilly breeze ruffled their petals. Through a lattice fence, I saw kids shooting basketball hoops in the back yard.

I was relieved. This place was actually OK. Celia Lee had really come through for Cody just like she'd promised. Now all I had to do was find her a decent foster family (ie not PODS related) until her mum got better. As missions go, it was unusually straightforward. I had no worries at all.

On my way in I passed a grumpy security guy flicking through one of those lurid shocker mags, like *My Stepmom is an Alien* or whatever. Another new kid was being shown over the home. She looked a lot like Sheridan, all emo-style hair and eyeliner. Maybe she could be a friend for Cody.

I found Cody in her room. She was by the window, watching the basketball players without seeing them. The charcoal-grey knitted beanie made her dark eyes seem even larger and more soulful.

It was strange meeting Cody Fortuna in person. I'd been kidding myself I already knew her, when all I really knew was snippets of personal history, not Cody the human being at all. I took deep breaths, centring myself so I could more easily tune into her vibe. Mr Allbright says that's the best guide to someone's state of mind.

Lonely, I thought. This girl was so absolutely lost it made me shiver. What was it she was needing and missing so badly? Did she even know?

I always get stage fright the first time I'm alone with a new human. Mr Allbright says this is normal. He says we have to remember this stuff WORKS. It's worked for aeons. To calm myself, I retied my boots and reminded myself of my original plan: to help Cody unlock her forgotten potential, inspiring her to become the magical girl she was always supposed to be. If an underachieving schoolgirl like me can become an angel, anything's possible, right? *Cody Fortuna is an angel in waiting*, I told myself. *She just doesn't know it yet.*

My first step was to stop her hiding away in her room. "Hi, sweetie," I said tentatively. "I'm your stand-in guardian angel. Hopefully you're feeling my vibes? I just spotted another new kid going into the social room. I think she'd be glad of some company."

I saw Cody's expression change. "Can't fester away in here my whole life," Cody muttered. "May as well meet some of the other losers."

I followed her down the corridor to the social room

where the new girl was flipping gloomily through TV channels. They eyed each other cautiously.

"Hi," said Emo Girl. "So what's this place like? It's a dump, right?"

Cody shrugged. "I've just been here like, two hours."

The girls started discussing music. They couldn't exactly go, "You know what? My life just fell apart." "Hey, mine too!" So they chatted awkwardly about Pink and Linkin Park.

The social room was as you'd expect, well-worn chairs and sofas, tired pot plants, curling movie posters, a pool-table. Then, *whoosh!* – it had a seven-foot-tall angel in it!

I was v. surprised! Surprised Ambriel had followed me to Bethesda AND that I was pleased to see him. Mostly, though, I was puzzled. Creation angels don't do one-to-one interaction with humans, the same way my angel buddies and I don't zoom around tinkering with Earth's biosphere or whatever. So what the sassafras was this hugely powerful cosmic being doing dropping into a children's home?

At this exact moment, actually, he was examining a drooping umbrella plant with the kind of horror I would personally reserve for the destruction of the rainforest. (Not to diss pot plants, but you can always buy another one, right?)

I saw Ambriel stretch out his hand. It was almost like he couldn't help it, like he was being pulled by the silent suffering of this v. common house plant. His long shimmery fingers softly touched the dull brittle leaves and I saw millions of green sparkles go into the plant. Just their colour alone made the room come more alive. I watched, holding my breath, as the ailing plant slowly straightened up from the roots, then *ping!* – out popped a crowd of vibey little shoots!

Ambriel gave a satisfied nod, then saw me and gave me a slightly embarrassed smile. I gave him a cheeky thumbs up. "Nice job, Ambriel!"

He seemed surprised that I'd used his name. He thought for a moment, then experimentally stuck up a giant shimmery thumb. I burst out laughing. A billion-year-old angel and he'd just cracked his first joke!

Seconds later we heard a ruckus in the foyer.

"I don't care if you've driven all the way from Timbuktu, lady! You can't leave that rust-bucket out front with the engine running. How do I know you don't have a ticking bomb in there?" It sounded like the security guy. Then I heard a female voice trying to smooth things over, maybe the director of the home.

Suddenly a young woman burst in. "Is Cody Fortuna in here?"

Cody looked alarmed. "Did I do something wrong?"

"You're Cody, right? We need you to help us out. You've got some..." the woman seemed to be struggling for the right words "...some visitors. We told them it's not a visiting day, and they need to go through the proper channels, but they say they've driven up from Arizona especially and they need to see you."

"But I don't know anyone in Arizona." Cody looked alarmed.

"Hey, *I'll* have 'em if she don't want 'em!" Emo Girl joked.

"If you could help us sort this out," the woman said anxiously. Cody and I followed her up to reception, my giant angel buddy tagging on behind. When she saw the three old ladies waiting at the desk, Cody stopped dead in her tracks.

To be strictly accurate, there was only one *really* old lady, plus two not *so* old but not exactly young either, ladies. I knew they had to be sisters; their wrinkly, apple-like faces were so spookily similar. It was like they were really all the same person, just at different stages. Through the open door I saw an ancient pick-up truck blasting out toxic exhaust fumes.

"Here, give me the keys! I'll turn off the fricking engine if you won't!" The security guy was turning brick-red with frustration.

"You do that, mister, and you'll be pushing us back to Arizona!" This was the oldest, fiercest lady who had more tattoos than Popeye. I didn't know old Native American ladies *got* tattoos, but then I hadn't pictured them wearing velour trackie bottoms either!

"We got battery problems," explained the youngest old lady. "It dies the minute it's switched off."

"I'm supposed to believe you drove all the way from the Navajo reservation and you didn't stop for gas?" The security guy snorted disbelievingly. "Is that some kind of Indian hoodoo?"

"We stopped for gas plenty times, mister," the fierce one flashed back. "As you mighta noticed we ain't so cute as we used to be. It's harder to sweet-talk truckers into giving us a jump start. We don't stop more than we have to. We just need to see Martin's girl, then we'll—"

The sisters suddenly clutched at each other. They had seen Cody. Their eyes thirstily drank her in. "That's her!" breathed the youngest old lady. "Oh, my stars! She's his spitting image!"

Cody went rigid with tension. What little colour there was in her cheeks drained away. "Who are you? How do you know my dad?"

The middle sister took a step towards Cody. "Honey, you ain't seen us since you were a little baby, but we're your aunts, your great aunts strictly speaking. This scary old hag is your Great Aunt Bonita, this is Great Aunt Jeannie, the baby of the family, and I'm the sane one, Great Aunt Evalina." Cody opened her mouth, but nothing came out.

"Ladies, it's wonderful that you came all this way to see your great niece," said the director smoothly. "Now I suggest you book yourselves into a nice motel, get in touch with the appropriate agencies, file the relevant paperwork; you might be able to visit her later in the week."

Aunt Bonita folded her arms. "Sugar, I'm seventy-eight years old. We've been on the road three days. I can't hardly tell day from night. I've drunk so much coffee I could get your security fella in a neck lock and not break a sweat. Don't tell me I can't see my kin because I will blow up worse than any of them terrorist devices you hear about." Cody looked awed and probably I did too!

How did they *know*? How could these old women know what had happened to their great niece when there had been no contact between the Navajo and Anglo sides of the family since Cody was two years old? And how did they know where to find her when she had just got here herself!

Without seeming to move, Aunt Bonita was

suddenly in arm's reach of Cody. She tweaked off her beanie and gave a funny little nod. "You've had that neatened up some since I last saw you."

Cody snatched back her hat. "The last time you saw me I was two, according to you!" she flashed.

"No, honey, Bonita saw you in a dream the other night," Aunt Jeannie said eagerly. "She saw you were in trouble and she called us both up to say we were driving up to Maryland to—"

"Jeannie, we got no time for chit-chat," Aunt Bonita interrupted. "We got a truck out there trying to shake itself to pieces." She fixed Cody with tiny glittering eyes. "We got a proposition for you. We want you to stay with us until your mama's fully recovered. Will you come?"

Cody looked as if a bomb had gone off in her head. Long-lost Navajo aunts who claim to have seen you in a dream and who drive through the night to rescue you – it's a lot to take in.

"You want me to come with you to the reservation?" she asked incredulously.

The aunts nodded simultaneously, looking like a set of très unusual car ornaments.

I could feel something in Cody being powerfully drawn to these eccentric old women. She'd been coping on her own for so long. Now, suddenly, someone wanted her; they'd actually gone out of their way to find her. But it was like coming out into too-bright sunshine after living too long in the dark. It was too much.

I knew she was going to turn them down and I thought she was right. She knew nothing about these old women. Plus, in my century, you can't just turn up at a children's home, declare you're a relative and take a child out of care. There are procedures, police checks, whatever – or there should be.

Next minute the reception area looked like it had been dropped into the blazing white-hot heart of a star. So much cosmic energy was circulating around Cody all of a sudden that my hair literally blew back from my face with the force.

I'm pretty hot at sending vibes these days, but I can't generate *that* much power, no trainee angel can. I turned to see what Ambriel made of all this. He gave me a calm thumbs up, like, s*orted*.

"That was *you*!" I was astounded. "Are you even supposed to USE that much cosmic energy on humans?"

The angel just pulled a face, like: *Pouf! Who cares about rules? We invented cosmic rules.*

WOOHOO! What a BLAST! cheered a voice from inner space. *That was ANGELTASTIC!* Attracted by the unusual cosmic activity Helix had come – or possibly been blown – online.

"Actually, it wasn't 'angeltastic', Helix," I said angrily. "Asking for TROUBLE, that's what that was! You'd better hope he didn't fry anyone's brains."

I couldn't believe Helix was being so irresponsible! Ambriel was used to dealing with oceans, forests, Earth's molten inner core and whatever. If you start throwing raw creation energy at human beings, you have to expect the unexpected. I *definitely* didn't expect what happened next as Cody took a tentative but life-changing step towards the aunts.

"I'll come," she said huskily. "Just till Mum's better though." Again I heard that annoying cheer from inner space.

"Well, thanks again for your support!" I snapped. A deranged angel turns your nice tidy plans upside down and stomps them into the ground, and your inner angel says it's a blast!

It took just a few phone calls to make the kind of complicated arrangements that normally take months. Finally Celia Lee came down to take the aunts' contact details. The children's home director seemed surprised to learn they had telephones on the reservation.

"Phones, microwave, satellite dish," Aunt Bonita reeled off carelessly. "Of course, being backward tribal folk, we got NO electricity to power them!"

Aunt Evalina shot her a nasty glare. "My sister has a

weird sense of humour," she apologised to the director. "The Navajo Nation's power supply ain't all it might be, but we got a back-up generator. Cody will have all the comforts she's used to."

Just like that it was settled. I was forced to hurry after Cody as she trundled her wheelie case towards the madly vibrating truck. Before I climbed inside, I turned to look for Ambriel, but having mashed up my mission and danced on the tiny little pieces he was nowhere to be seen.

Just go with the flow, Helix said serenely. *It'll be fine.* What I said back to Helix is not repeatable.

Aunt Bonita put her foot down and we roared out into oncoming traffic to angry hoots from the other motorists. *If you want the Universe to laugh out loud...* I thought bitterly.

Mr Allbright says we will eventually learn that some missions take on an uncanny life of their own from the beginning. He says you should always start out with a game plan, but sometimes you just have to chuck it away, climb on board and let the Universe carry you where it wants you to go.

I blew out my breath. It seemed like the Universe was working from an unnecessarily complicated script if you asked me: interfering Creation angels, and a road trip into the Arizona desert with Navajo aunts –

from the same family that allegedly put Cody and her mum under a curse...

Feeling *très* stressed, I fired off a text to Sam explaining that Cody's rellies had shown up and we were unexpectedly *en route* to the Navajo reservation. As I pressed SEND I had a sudden mad flash of hope. Maybe they'd decided Cody didn't need me. Then I could fly off to the Himalayas to join the search party for Reuben.

Sam's reply pinged back in a matter of seconds: Advise u 2 stay w the programme til furth notice.

I was like, thanks a LOT, Sam. Whose programme would that be exactly? It would be REALLY good to know.

Meanwhile, as any angel could have predicted, the humans were crashing down from Ambriel's massive cosmic high. Cody looked utterly freaked by what she'd done. Aunt Bonita just seemed determined to pick a fight.

"You and your mama lived in Potomac, right?" she shot at Cody. Cody gave a tight little nod.

"You realise that town was built on stolen Indian land? And inside those pretty fancy houses what football team do you think those rich white men support? The Washington Redskins! Ha!" Cody's aunt banged on the steering wheel for emphasis like she'd scored a point.

"I never actually thought about it," Cody admitted stiffly.

Aunt Bonita was quiet for a few seconds then she began to sing in a screechy voice, using notes I never would have imagined any human (not in severe pain) could produce, like, "*HEYA HEYA HEYA HEYA!!!*"

You could see Cody sliding down in her seat, probably willing herself to be invisible to the startled motorists. Aunt Bonita gave a witchy laugh which turned into a rattling smoker's cough. "You don't like your people's music, Cody?"

"What music?" snapped Aunt Evalina. "All the child can hear is you wailing like a *chiindi!*"

"Roll me a cigarette," Aunt Bonita ordered her. "I can't find the Beltway without some fresh nicotine in my bloodstream."

"Let one of us drive then if you're so tired and cranky," Aunt Jeannie complained. "Doesn't make sense to drag us all the way from Arizona, then hog the driver's seat yourself."

"Bonita's a control freak," Aunt Evalina announced. "Always was."

"You shouldn't force your passengers to breathe your smoke." Cody's voice was shaky but defiant. "You could give them cancer."

The aunts gawped at her as if she'd just sprouted

horns. Aunt Bonita couldn't speak she was so shocked. When Aunt Jeannie recovered, she said quietly, "Cody, in our culture what you did just then was very insulting. Navajo children never talk back to their elders. It's not your fault, honey. You've been brought up by white people. You never had nobody to teach you good manners. We understand that and now we've explained, I'm sure we won't need to speak of it again."

Aunt Evalina made a soft grunt of agreement. Cody had flushed dark red to her ears. Aunt Bonita stared stonily at the road ahead. Neither of them spoke.

"Now who wants candy?" Aunt Jeannie asked brightly.

CHAPTER ELEVEN

We were sitting at a gas station, waiting for Aunt Jeannie and Aunt Evalina to come out of Dunkin' Donuts. We were technically at a standstill, but with the engine running, the aunts' ancient truck was rocking and shuddering, as if it just might go roaring off to Arizona on its own. While we waited I composed a new text to Reuben: The Agency wil find u, so stay strong. Wish I ws with ur srch party, not stuck in a truck with 3 crazy women.

Once, on our soul-retrieval mission, Reubs saved the whole situation with a smile. *He couldn't be gone.* How could he be gone when I could hear his husky, teasing voice inside my head as clear as day?

Please don't let the PODS have got him, I prayed with a pang of terror.

To stop myself going mad with worry, I tried calling Lola. She should have arrived in the Himalayas by now. But her phone was switched off and I just got a perky message.

"Open the door. I'm dropping the damn Doritos!" Aunt Evalina was suddenly glowering at Aunt Bonita through the open window. Cody's great aunts had seemed fiercely united in their mission to rescue her, but now they had Cody they were snapping and sulking like seven-year-olds; except seven-year-olds don't generally chain-smoke.

The aunts squabbled all the way from Maryland through the state of Tennessee, meanwhile working their way through shedloads of junk food. They kept offering snacks to Cody, but she silently shook her head. Now and then she sipped at a diet Coke.

"That stuff rots your innards," Aunt Bonita growled, exhaling clouds of smoke into the truck.

"The child's queasy, leave her be," Aunt Evalina told her. She started flicking through the radio stations till she found a country music tune to hum along to. But after so many days on the road, even the aunts' caffeine-fuelled energy levels were dropping. After three choruses of "Achy Breaky Heart", their voices petered out. By the time we reached Nashville and drove by the Grand Old Opry, the world famous country music venue, I was the only person who actually bothered to look.

We stayed the night in a motel where the decor was stuck in a 1970s time warp. Giant lime green and orange flowers loomed from every surface, making the room more claustrophobic than it already was. Cody fell asleep as soon as her head hit the pillow. Aunt Evalina and Aunt Jeannie were close behind.

Aunt Bonita propped herself up on top of the lime and orange bedcover, her bare feet stuck out stiffly in front, her eyes glinting beadily in the light of the TV, as she watched CNN news with the sound down.

A terrible flood had made millions of people homeless. The snows in the Himalayas were melting faster than anyone had predicted...

Before I left I'd hastily downloaded Reuben's tunes. I put in my iPod (just one ear-bud because I was on duty) and clicked on another of Reubs' works in progress, "Earth Dreams".

Reuben has this way of mixing shimmering cosmic chords with gritty human beats borrowed from tunes I've lent him. His voice isn't totally tuneful, but as a sound it works. When he reached the chorus, I broke into goosebumps as he sang:

Born from the same star, you've come so far,
Born from the same star, you've come so far,
But the circle got broken, Earth was torn open,
All her treasures stolen, and this wasn't,
this wasn't, this wasn't what we dreamed...

How the sassafras had Ambriel's words, which he never at *any* point spoke aloud, found their way into Reuben's tune!!

I felt as if I was balanced on the edge of some huge mystery. Lola's glimpse of a nightmare future, Ambriel's last-ditch crusade to save the world, a Navajo girl under a curse; they were all connected, I could feel it – if I could only figure out how...

I could hear some kind of disturbance in the hall, probably guests coming back late after a few beers, but Aunt Bonita was instantly on red alert.

She glanced sharply at Cody, uneasily asleep on the pull-out bed provided for kids, then with a tiny grunt of effort, she swung her legs off the bed. She softly dragged a chair over to the door and jammed it carefully under the handle. Then she went back to CNN. Apparently Aunt Bonita was planning to sit up all night guarding her great niece.

I wondered what this feisty old Navajo lady could have seen in her dream that made her drive hell for leather all the way to Maryland? It wasn't possible, surely, that she knew about the PODS? If she knew what Cody was up against, she'd know that just blocking a motel door wouldn't stop them. The Powers of Darkness can send a disembodied agent swirling up through a bathroom plughole if they want to. They could be monitoring us from the Hell dimensions right now through the screen of the TV...

Stop it! I commanded. *You're freaking yourself out.*

I was totally freaked for a few seconds, then I pulled myself together and got busy with some cosmic precautions of my own. I moved softly around the room setting shimmery angelic symbols on the ceiling, floor, walls, door and windows. These ancient symbols are invisible to humans and blazingly toxic to the PODS.

As I drew the final symbol, sealing the circle of divine protection, I caught sight of Aunt Bonita's lips moving in silent prayer and wondered if I'd got it all wrong. Maybe Aunt Bonita *did* know who was threatening Cody. Maybe she was doing the only thing a human can do: whisper a prayer and stay on guard till morning.

CHAPTER TWELVE

Next morning Aunt Bonita grudgingly allowed Aunt Evalina to take over the driving seat. She claimed her rheumatism was playing up, but I thought the old lady was simply worn out from sitting up guarding Cody, on top of three days' solid driving.

We had another long drive ahead of us if we were going to reach Dallas by nightfall. Hopefully we'd make it to Arizona by sometime tomorrow.

Cody looked dazed and pale. She never seemed particularly well, but today she looked like she might keel over in her seat.

Having sat beside her for hours in the cramped, smoke-filled cab of a pick-up truck, I was getting to know her vibes. It seemed like the right moment to dig a little deeper, before we reached the reservation where I'd have to deal with all kinds of unknown factors. Extremely gently, as Mr Allbright taught us, I sent out a teensy bit of my own energy into the first outer layer of Cody's energy field.

As I suspected, she was physically in bad shape. I had a feeling she might have an allergy the doctors hadn't picked up. Next layer down I found a faithful record of Cody's recent emotions. They were what you'd expect: worry for her mum, intense anxiety that she might not be allowed to live with her again. In the third layer I found worries about school, friends, boys. Normal teen worries.

Four layers down I found energy so stagnant, so totally disconnected from Cody, that I actually recoiled. It felt *wrong*, like a seam of hard black coal where there should be sparkly little streams. We'd studied energy blockages in class. Mr Allbright says sometimes it's so painful to humans to be who they really are, they simply shut off huge areas of their life force without even knowing. Some humans, he told us, run on as little as *twenty per cent* of their energy supply!

I wished Mr Allbright was here with me now to explain my disturbing discovery. The feelings she'd buried were too huge, too traumatic, to be explained away by the loss of a parent she'd never really known. I've been an angel for long enough now to know that the PODS are not responsible for every single painful thing that happens to a human child. Sometimes stuff just happens. But when it does, the Dark Agencies are always ready and waiting, invisibly nudging things along, playing on human weaknesses, sneaking ugly thoughts into people's heads, hoping to turn a crisis into a complete catastrophe.

"I'm going to throw up!" Cody said abruptly. We had to stop a couple more times before we reached the next official gas station, where she stumbled to the washroom, looking absolutely white.

While she was gone, Aunt Evalina checked in her battered plastic wallet. "The good news is we can afford to fill up with gas another couple of times," she announced. "The bad news is if we want to eat, we'll have to sleep in the truck."

Around ten o'clock that evening they stopped off at a Spanish-style roadside diner. The aunts ordered tacos. Cody leaned back with her eyes closed, sipping her iced water. Then everyone catnapped in the truck until first light.

Next day Aunt Jeannie took over the driving. The pick-up was in serious trouble by this time, speeds over 30 mph made it rattle like a bag of nails. When clouds of steam started curling out from under the bonnet, they were finally forced to pull off the road.

Aunt Evalina said someone would have to walk to the next town and find a mechanic. Aunt Bonita said something v. rude in Navajo and demanded to be let out of the truck. She stalked stiffly around the steaming truck as vehicles whizzed past, dangerously close. She began to chant loudly in Navajo.

Cody was cringing at the looks from passing motorists. "What's she *doing*?"

"She's blessing the truck," Aunt Jeannie explained.

"Or scaring it!" Aunt Evalina let out a snicker of laughter. "That old bootface sure scares the hell outa me!"

As she chanted, Cody's aunt took several pinches of something from a small leather pouch, sprinkling them carefully around the truck. I noticed her carefully sprinkle in all four directions: north, south, east and west. Finally she touched her pinched fingertips to her crown, then to her lips. Then, slightly out of breath, she got back in the truck.

"Start her up!" she commanded.

Cody's eyes widened in amazement as the truck roared into life. "It stopped steaming! You didn't even put in water!"

"Should get us home," said Aunt Bonita casually. "Jim Yellowbird can fix her when we get back."

"What's that stuff in the pouch – like, *magic dust*?"

Cody couldn't admit it even to herself, but she was totally spooked.

"Pollen," said Aunt Bonita, lighting a new ciggie.

"You fixed a truck with *pollen*?"

"I can't fix nothin'," Aunt Bonita said calmly. "I BLESSED the truck and the Holy People graciously decided to help us out."

"The Holy People? Who are *they*?" Cody looked like she'd fallen into Looking Glass Land.

"They created our world," Aunt Jeannie explained in the matter-of-fact tone she'd used when Aunt Bonita was blessing the truck. I hadn't heard of the Holy People either until that moment, but I knew they were real. I'd felt a shimmery hum of power building around the truck as Aunt Bonita asked for their help.

I'm a total newbie when it comes to identifying the different hierarchies of divine beings; angels, archangels, saints, gods and goddesses, that's as far as I feel confident. But the Holy People's vibes seemed oddly similar to Ambriel's. I wondered if they were like, distant Navajo cousins to Creation angels?

Thanks to the combined efforts of Aunt Bonita and the Holy People, the truck drove like a dream for the rest of the journey.

As we zoomed across the border of New Mexico into

the state of Arizona, Aunt Bonita suddenly cleared her throat. "We'll soon be arriving in Dinétah."

Cody looked baffled. "I thought we were going to Navajoland."

"Dinétah means the land of the Diné," Aunt Evalina explained. "Diné is another name for the Navajo. It just means 'people'."

"Young people nowadays just call it the Rez," Aunt Jeannie said, beaming.

Aunt Bonita frowned, not appreciating her younger sisters' interruptions. "When we get to the reservation, Cody, some things are going to seem strange to you," she went on grimly. "Try not to judge us. Act respectful. To understand why our people act and think like they do, you need to know what they've been through over the centuries."

Cody flinched as if she was waiting for the dentist's drill. "Like what?"

"I'm seventy-eight," Aunt Bonita told her. "I don't have enough years left on this Earth to tell you all the things white people did to us. I'll just tell you about the Long Walk."

"OK," Cody said reluctantly. I think she felt that her aunt was accusing her personally.

Aunt Bonita was staring off into the distance. Her expression was suddenly utterly bleak. "In 1864, for reasons too complicated to go into now, the US government decided to move the Navajo people off their ancestral land, the home where we had lived in peace and harmony for centuries. They sent us to a place called Basque Redondo, three hundred miles away in Mexico."

"Three hundred miles isn't so far," Cody said.

"It's a long way on foot," Aunt Evalina said quietly. "If you were a half-starved little five-year-old, or old and frail, or heavily pregnant, or sick with fever."

"The journey took eighteen days." Aunt Bonita seemed to be watching the ordeal unspooling in her head. "Two hundred Navajo died on the way. We lived in exile for many years. Thousands died from starvation or from the white man's many diseases, or maybe just because our hearts were broken. The Navajo people almost died out."

Aunt Bonita turned to Cody with a grim smile. "Then one day the government agreed to let the tattered remains of our tribe return home. They didn't give back *all* our land, just the poorest, driest, most hard-scrabble part. Only now they had a new name for it. They called it 'the Indian Reservation'. They herded us on to it like prisoners, and told us we weren't allowed to leave."

"Navajo people didn't win the right to travel outside the reservation till 1924!" Aunt Jeannie chipped in.

Cody looked as if her head was spinning. "I don't get

it," she said, bewildered. "The land belonged to you."

"You got that the wrong way round, honey," Aunt Evalina corrected. "That's how white people think. This land doesn't belong to us. We belong to the land. When we go away, it suffers. When we return, it welcomes us like our mother."

"Look out of the window, Cody," Aunt Jeannie said softly. "Dinétah is welcoming you now."

Maybe it was Aunt Jeannie's absolute belief that what she was saying was true, but I suddenly seemed able to see this barren landscape as the aunts saw it. This empty desert was alive! The heatwaves rising off the road, the cries of birds, the desert wind bending back thousands of feathery wild grasses; everything sang, *Welcome home!*

We drove on the dusty back roads for hours. I was just starting to think we'd never get there when the aunts raised a loud cheer as a sign loomed up at the side of the road.

YOU ARE ENTERING NAVAJOLAND – KEEP OUT!

The aunts started chatting and laughing, pointing out landmarks to Cody. They hung out of the windows, sniffing the dry, pine-scented air like wild ponies. Relief shone from their faces. I realised some of their sniping had been pure tension. Away from the reservation, they'd been fishes out of water. Now they were home.

The sun was almost setting as Aunt Jeannie turned off

the main road and we went bumping and bouncing down a rutted dirt track. On one side was a shallow creek reflecting the fading pinks and golds; on the other a canyon wall rose up like a fortress. Unfamiliar birds called from perches too high to see. An owl, silent as a cloud, swooped across the truck, making Cody jump. We passed another sign: GHOST CANYON.

Ghost Canyon was basically a stretched-out string of scattered dwellings. Some were just ramshackle trailers apparently parked at random. Some were those wooden houses that arrive all in one piece on the back of a truck. Almost all these homes had additional roundish, earth-coloured dwellings built close by. Aunt Jeannie said they were *hogans*, traditional Navajo houses. "Nowadays Navajo people tend not to live in them; we use them more for celebrations or ceremonies."

"Butterfly Woman lives in a *hogan*," Aunt Evalina contradicted.

"Butterfly Woman is a dying breed," Aunt Jeannie said, then looked like she could have bitten off her tongue.

There was a v. sticky silence, then Aunt Evalina started chatting about the sheep we could see grazing outside the houses. "They're blue *churros*, originally brought here by the Spanish. We use their wool to weave rugs and blankets."

Cody was suddenly craning forward, looking confused. "Didn't there used to be ponies over there?" The aunts exchanged pleased glances that Cody had finally remembered something about her father's home.

"Do you know how to ride?" asked Aunt Evalina.

Cody nodded eagerly. "Mom worked as a housekeeper for a while. I helped out in the stables, and they let me ride the ponies."

"She's part Navajo, of course she can ride," Aunt Bonita said gruffly. "We'll get Earl Brokeshoulder on to it. He'll find you a pony."

I'd assumed Cody was a townie like me. I'd never pictured her on horseback. I realised I was seeing a new side of Cody, one I never would have seen if we'd followed my original plan. For the first time it occurred to me that Ambriel might actually have known what he was doing. Unfortunately he wasn't here to ask.

The truck abruptly swerved down another narrower track, almost immediately stopping in a spurt of dust and gravel. For once I was actually glad to be invisible so no one could see my expression. We'd pulled up outside a shabby old trailer that seemed to have been dumped down in the middle of a junkyard: old tyres, ancient electrical appliances, broken sofas with the metal springs exploding from their seats, a rusting ride-on mower, a truck minus its wheels, used to store hay.

Picking their way through the junk were goats, hens and a few of the famous blue *churro* sheep. Several dogs ran up to greet us, tongues lolling. Off in the trees I saw three or four smaller trailers, each one in its own spreading circle of chaos.

"You're staying here with Bonita," Aunt Evalina explained. "Jeannie and me live in those trailers over there. We're constantly in and out of each other's homes so you'll still see us plenty."

Cody's horror was written all over her face. *Nowhere to run.*

CHAPTER THIRTEEN

Getting out of the truck, Cody stumbled, falling on to gravel and bruising her knees. She was totally exhausted from her epic journey. Even worse, she was in shock. She'd remembered cute Navajo ponies. She hadn't remembered that her relatives lived in a total tip.

I was surprised to hear a hum of voices coming from Aunt Bonita's trailer. A woman said in Navajo, "It's them! I heard the truck!"

"You could hear that truck coming in Ship Rock!" someone joked.

"Sounds like your welcome party got here early!" Aunt Evalina gave her niece a resigned grin.

Cody had been rubbing her hurt knee through her

jeans. She looked up in panic. "You didn't say I'd have to meet people!"

"We know you're tired, Cody," Aunt Bonita said briskly, "but your dad was well respected around here. It means a lot to folks in Ghost Canyon to know Martin's daughter has finally come back."

"I'm *not* back though!" Cody's voice sounded shrill.

"Everybody understands you're just visiting, honey," Aunt Jeannie said quickly. "Just smile and say hi. You don't need to make a speech!"

Cody followed her aunts inside, looking ready to pass out with nerves. Inside the trailer Navajo people of all ages stood, leaned or perched anywhere they could find space. The men wore jeans and T-shirts. I was tickled to see some of the older men had on big black cowboy hats. They all wore Navajo jewellery – rings, heavy silver bangles, or some kind of Navajo talisman round their necks. The women wore traditional bunchy skirts and blouses with velvet ribbons stitched to the seams. Over the blouses they wore elaborate necklaces of silver and turquoise. (Later I saw the same women in the local supermarket wearing trackie bottoms and realised they'd put on their traditional finery in Cody's honour.)

When the assembled guests saw Cody, I heard soft exclamations. Some of the women's eyes went shiny with tears.

"OK, you've seen her, now let's eat," joked an old man whose faded T-shirt advertised an old rodeo in Santa Fe. "You all brought enough food to feed a starving nation!"

Women quickly stripped clingfilm from pies, puddings, breads and whatever else people had brought to celebrate Cody's arrival. The aunts wove in and out of the guests, introducing their niece to people with average American-type surnames like Johnson and others with obviously Indian names like Manybeads and Bitterwater.

The old man who had taken the heat off Cody turned out to be Jim Yellowbird, who ran Ghost Canyon's only garage. Like the other older men he wore his long grey hair in a ponytail under his broad-brimmed hat. He listened patiently as Cody's aunt listed her recent problems with the truck. "I'll get her up on the ramp as soon as I can," he promised.

He turned to Cody who was still looking like she wished the ground would open up and swallow her. "Ghost Canyon is kinda quiet," he explained, smiling. "You're the closest thing we got to a celebrity. In a week or two everything will just simmer down and folks will simply accept you."

He was just trying to put Cody at ease, but I wasn't sure what he said was true. I'd heard some guests making malicious comments.

"What happened to her *hair*? Is that some white fashion?"

"Did you see how she looked Jim Yellowbird right in the face? No Navajo child would be that rude!"

"She can't even speak our language!"

"I wouldn't allow those boots in my house!"

"You know her mother's sick in the head?"

"Why are they so sure it's *this* child?"

The aunts gave no sign of hearing these mutterings. They probably didn't want to spoil Cody's welcome by causing a scene. Then suddenly Aunt Bonita had had enough. Marching over to the rumour-mongers she let loose a ferocious stream of Navajo. The only sentence I understood was, "Dolores Bitterwater – you should be ashamed!" The rest of her speech was too fast and furious to follow.

Four people, including Dolores Bitterwater, left immediately, shooting dark looks at Cody. Cody couldn't understand what they said, but she caught the vibe and flushed up to her ears.

Once Cody's ill-wishers had gone, the party settled down into a normal Navajo gathering: plates of food being passed around, little kids dashing round sneaking cakes when no one was looking, women chatting about WeightWatchers, men discussing the prospects of the Arizona Cardinals, the local football team.

One obviously pregnant teenage girl was bottle-feeding a toddler as she discussed names with her friend. "I want to call her Tara. It goes really well with Tazbah." She patted her daughter's chubby knee. "I found it on a website. It means 'star'."

I heard Aunt Evalina give a weary sigh. "If Roxie put as much effort into choosing her babies' fathers as she does picking out their names," she muttered to Aunt Jeannie.

Roxie and the other girls slid narrow-eyed looks at Cody. The boys looked at her too, but in a different way.

To Cody's obvious relief Aunt Bonita called her over. "Come and meet Earl. He says he knows where he can find you a pony." I was startled to see that Earl wore a gun holster strapped to his waist, then realised his brown short-sleeved shirt was part of his uniform. Earl was a cop with the Navajo tribal police.

"Hi, you must be the famous Cody Fortuna," he said, holding out his hand. "I'm Earl Brokeshoulder and this is—"

"I'm Lily Topaha!" A sharp-faced young woman had followed Earl in. She was dressed American-style in shirt and jeans, apart from her Navajo jewellery. She had on so much ethnic silver and turquoise she literally jingled every time she inhaled.

"I'm late for a meeting," she gushed, "but I had to

come and meet you on your first day. Welcome home, Cody. I'm just SO happy you found your way back to us!"

Cody looked appalled. "Oh! No, I'm not really—"

"We have a lot in common." Lily sounded breathless and fierce all at once. "We were both stolen from our people at exactly the same age."

"I *wasn't* stolen from any *people*! My mum and dad *separated*, OK?" It was the closest I'd seen Cody get to being genuinely angry.

Lily just steamed on regardless. "You know what they call us in the tribe? *Lost birds*. But we're coming back, Cody. The lost birds are returning one by one."

"Lily!" Earl's voice was polite but firm. "Cody's tired. The lost bird talk can keep." He gave Cody an apologetic smile. "Nice to meet you, kiddo. I'll be in touch about the pony."

"See you *very* soon, Cody," Lily promised. I could hear her jewellery jingling like sleigh bells all the way to the car. Cody waited until the car drove off then fled outside. Aunt Evalina and I both went after her.

"You have to try to forgive Lily," her aunt said. "She's so busy making up for all that lost time, she can be insensitive. I'm sorry."

"I'm just here till my mom is out of the hospital," Cody said in a tight voice. "I'm not anyone's lost bird. I'm not a Navajo. Even my dad was only part Navajo."

Aunt Evalina sighed. "No offence, Cody, but that's how white people think. 'Half this. Quarter that.' Time was, you just needed one Indian somewhere in your family tree to count as Indian, not even that if you'd been brought up inside the tribe. Unfortunately, these days, even Navajo people get on their high horses and need you to prove your tribal credentials."

"I don't have to prove my credentials." Cody was trembling now. "I don't belong here. I *never* belonged here."

"Where *do* you belong then, honey?" Evalina asked quietly.

Cody stared around her in obvious dismay before she said despairingly, "Nowhere, I guess."

Later Aunt Evalina came into the curtained cubicle where Cody was pretending to sleep. "You *belong*, do you hear me?" she said fiercely. "You belong to the Navajo people." Cody didn't move.

"You belong to us," Aunt Evalina repeated, "and you belong to this *land*, Cody, to these canyons and mountains. In Navajo we say, 'The wind knows your name.'"

I remembered how the windblown plants had seemed joyful as we passed. Did the wind in Navajoland truly recognise this lost girl? If so, the Earth was more magical than I'd ever dreamed.

"Your great-great-grandmothers and their great-great-grandmothers walked this country before you." Aunt Evalina was still talking in the same low fierce voice. "They knew the plants and the seasons. They knew how to walk in harmony with the Earth. We call this way of living *Hozho*, the Blessing Way. Everything in harmony, Cody, all living things balanced in perfect harmony."

Cody pulled her pillow over her head. Either she couldn't stand to hear any more Navajo talk or she was crying. Aunt Evalina hovered for a while then went back to her sisters.

I heard Aunt Bonita give a snort of laughter. "That poor girl's racking her brains trying to figure out what the Blessing Way has to do with that mountain of junk she saw when she pulled up here, after driving across America with the three old bats from hell."

"Who are you calling an old bat?" demanded Evalina. There was a soft *flump* as if someone had thrown a cushion.

"Did you see how uncomfortable Cody was with everyone?" Aunt Jeannie sounded distressed.

"Her *retarded* relatives." Aunt Bonita's voice was gritty with pain. "That's what her mama said."

"Don't blame Julia for that," begged Aunt Jeannie. "We could all see she was sick even then."

"Sick but not stupid," said Aunt Bonita. "Seeing her

husband's people living through one catastrophe after another. Why would she want her child mixed up in that, if she had a choice?"

"That's ALL Julia saw," Aunt Evalina protested. "People on welfare, drunks, junkies, broken people barely surviving."

Aunt Bonita said very quietly, "I worry that just barely surviving is all our people got left. Bringing Cody back, seeing the reservation through her eyes – it's not an uplifting sight."

"Were we wrong to fetch her?" Aunt Evalina asked unhappily.

Aunt Bonita's voice dropped almost to a whisper. "No, she's our only chance..." Her voice trailed away.

"But—" prompted Aunt Jeannie.

"We got a glimmer of hope." Aunt Bonita said huskily. "That don't mean we'll get what we pray for."

I suddenly needed some space. Shimmering out through the trailer, I stood shivering under the stars, trying to make sense of what I'd just heard.

I hadn't been keen for Cody to go with the aunts, as you know. But when they invited Cody to stay with them, I had sensed that their concern was genuine. I still believed that. At the motel Aunt Bonita seemed convinced Cody was in some kind of imminent danger. Now it looked as if concern for their niece wasn't the only reason they'd wanted to spring Cody from the children's home. It almost seemed like they needed her to do something for *them*. Why else would Aunt Bonita say she was their only chance?

Apart from the murmur of voices inside the trailer, everything was silent. I looked up at the stars and felt like little Navajo children must have felt through the centuries: so much awesome beauty casually scattered across the dark. What was it even *for*? I felt a pang, wishing Reuben was with me to share this sight.

I remembered a story Aunt Jeannie had told Cody on the road about Coyote the trickster. The animals were fed up with not being able to see after dark, so the Holy People agreed to set lights in the sky by night as well as by day. First they created a moon from a large pearly shell. Then they got to work on the constellations, searching the riverbed for thousands of smooth, shiny pebbles. They'd intended to arrange the stones to form shimmery, cosmic-type pictures, but they couldn't agree on a final design. Coyote listened to the Holy People arguing for a while, then totally lost patience and flung the remaining stars up into the sky just anyhow! That's why some stars make patterns and others are like, completely random.

As I gazed up at the starlit sky, praying that Reuben was safe, every single tiny hair rose up on the back of my neck. I'd been alone. Now, suddenly, I wasn't. Ghostly voices rose and fell on the desert wind in an ancient chant I'd heard before:

House made of dawn
House made of evening
House built of pollen
In beauty may I walk
Beauty above me
Beauty below me
Beauty behind me
In beauty may I walk...

In that moment, my mind suddenly connected up the dots. *Hozho*, the Navajo Blessing Way, where animals, humans and divine beings coexisted in harmony, was the exact same world the Creation angels dreamed into being! I looked back at the trailer in its sea of rusting household appliances, and for the first time I really grasped what the Navajo – what *humans* – had lost.

I felt that sighing, golden breath, as if Ambriel had just been waiting for me to understand.

Inside the trailer someone started to scream.

CHAPTER FOURTEEN

Cody's aunts weren't the most cuddly human beings on the planet, but they were totally brilliant in a crisis. They stayed absolutely cool and calm.

Aunt Evalina filled hot-water bottles and put them under Cody's covers. (Cody's tiny room was suddenly as clammy as an underground cellar.) Aunt Bonita burned strong-smelling herbs, wafting healing fumes around the tiny room. Aunt Jeannie stroked Cody's forehead, chanting softly in Navajo.

While the aunts worked flat out to heal Cody on the human plane, I steadily pushed up the Light levels. It felt good: three humans and an angel working side by side to defeat the Dark Agencies, each of us doing what we did best.

Obviously I knew who was behind it. I knew the moment I walked in. The chill clammy air, the pulsing terror you could almost taste, the stomach-turning smell that was worse than bad drains. They might as well have spray-painted the walls on their way out: PODS RULE.

I was furious with myself. If I'd followed basic cosmic protection procedure as soon as we arrived, they wouldn't have got within miles. *Great guardian angel you are*, I thought. But this wasn't the time to beat myself up.

Cody screamed and screamed and screamed like she was on some high scary ledge all alone. When someone's in the grip of night terrors, they're completely beyond your reach, deaf and blind to everything but their fear.

As the Light levels crept up, together with the herbs and chanting, the toxic vibes were gradually banished. Cody's body temperature improved, and her screaming eventually died to a whimper. Her eyelids flickered as she murmured something I couldn't catch, then, instead of waking, she slipped into a deep, dreamless sleep.

While she slept, I did what I should have done from the start. I ran outside and wove a shimmery net of angelic protection symbols around the trailer. Then I went back inside and boosted the Light levels so high Aunt Bonita's prayer plants literally grew six centimetres overnight!

I was overdoing it and I didn't care. I'd promised the Agency to take care of Cody and I'd let her down. I should have been on it a hundred per cent, but I'd let myself get distracted by my own personal worries. It wouldn't happen again. Next time the PODS came (and I had no doubt there would be a next time) I'd be ready.

Meanwhile I had some serious thinking to do. For the first time since I started angel school I took Mr Allbright's advice and actually *used* my notebook, noting anything that puzzled me to mull over later.

At the top of the first page I wrote:

Aunts! Why did they bring Cody back to the Rez?

Underneath I wrote:

PODS!!! They tried to keep Cody and her rellies apart. Why?

Finally I scribbled:

What has Cody got to do with Ambriel's dream?

I closed my notebook, hugging it in my arms, as if that would magically transform these riddles into answers. I had no clue why this vulnerable girl was causing so much cosmic excitement, but I was determined to find out.

Next day Cody showed no sign of remembering what had happened. She actually seemed in an unusually relaxed mood, possibly due to all our combined efforts. Her face even had some colour.

She pitched in to help her aunts put a brunch together from the left-over party food. For the first time I saw her eat with genuine enjoyment. "I remember this bread!" she said, surprised. "I used to love it. What's it called again?"

"Navajo Kneeldown bread!" Aunt Jeannie sounded pleased. "It was your dad's favourite too when he was a little boy."

After the meal the aunts took Cody for a walk through the canyon. Cody kept stopping to gaze about her. So did I. You know when you meet someone who is utterly and unreasonably beautiful? There's no one thing you can put your finger on, but they totally blow you away. The canyon was like that. The light, the air scented with plants I couldn't identify, the glowing pink and red colours in the sandstone.

I saw Cody suddenly let out her breath. It was like, here, in her father's land, she could finally breathe. The aunts let her take it all in in her own way, occasionally telling her names of plants: Indian paintbrush, larkspur, sagebrush, showing her coyote tracks.

At the same time they were subtly feeding Cody titbits of Navajo info. I don't know about Cody, but I couldn't always tell if the aunts were describing an actual event in history, a long ago family memory or some old legend. I'm not sure if they even saw a difference.

"Everything Mother Earth has to give us is right here in Navajoland," Aunt Jeannie said, beaming at Cody. "Canyons, forests, lakes and deserts, rivers, sun, wind and snow. She gives us medicine and food and she shares her sacred teachings."

"I don't mean to be rude, but I don't understand how the Earth can teach you anything," Cody said shyly.

Aunt Bonita frowned. "Because you still don't believe the Earth is alive."

The aunts had brought along large canvas bags. As they walked and talked, they stopped to collect leaves. "See how we never take more than a few leaves from each plant?" Aunt Evalina said. "Then they'll come again next year."

"Our people eat a lot of wild food," Aunt Jeannie chipped in. "Corn silk, wild onions, bee weed. We grow our own corn. We don't go to the supermarket more than we have to."

"My mom practically has a panic attack every time she sees the supermarket bill," said Cody. "She's like, 'How is that possible? We bought like, FIVE items!'"

"How is your mom?" Aunt Bonita sounded casual as she tipped back her head to look at the cloudless sky.

"You weren't on the phone this morning above five minutes."

"She didn't want to run up your bill," Cody said quickly. "She's fine. She'll be home in no time!" There was no home for Julia or Cody since Elliot kicked Cody out, but no one liked to say this aloud.

Aunt Evalina suddenly smacked herself on the side of the head. "Bonita, I forgot to tell you! Nettie called. She needs to borrow the truck. She says let her know when it's fixed and she won't need to keep it more than a week."

Aunt Bonita just said placidly, "OK."

Cody looked shocked. "You're letting someone use the truck for a whole week! What if you need to go somewhere?"

Aunt Evalina smiled. "When someone needs something, we give it; that's the Navajo way."

"The old way," Jeannie corrected. "Times are changing."

Aunt Bonita stopped to examine a clump of flowering plants. They looked like miniature sunflowers, tiny enough to plant round a doll's house. Their sharp-edged grey leaves bristled with tiny hairs. Cody's aunt bent stiff knees to look closer. She clicked her tongue. "These are flowering way too early. I doubt they'll come up again next year." Aunt Bonita hunted around until she found a sturdy stick. She began digging around the roots of one of the plants, which hadn't yet come into bud.

"I'm gonna plant this one where I can keep an eye on it. It might take, it might not." She pulled a wad of clean tissues from her pocket. "Run to the creek and give these a good soaking," she told Cody.

She carefully lifted out the plant with its tiny hairy rootball. I sent the plant a zap of angelic energy to help it survive the move. (I'd become a LOT more eco-minded thanks to Ambriel.)

Cody came back with the sodden tissues. "I don't get it!" She sounded almost accusing. "It's not *your* fault if they die. You can't look after like, every single plant in Ghost Canyon."

Aunt Bonita was wrapping the damp tissues around the roots. "True," she agreed, brushing dirt off her knees, "but I can try to save this one. We should be heading back," she told her sisters. "Jim said he might be over to pick up the truck."

On the way back Cody kept turning round to gaze back the way they'd come. There was something new in her eyes, a light that hadn't been there before.

Back in the trailer Aunt Bonita told Cody to wash the grit out of the leaves they'd gathered on their walk, then she threw the washed leaves into a pan of boiling water, leaving them to simmer. A powerful herbal smell gradually filled the trailer.

"Is that for supper?" Cody asked doubtfully.

Aunt Bonita gave her witchy laugh. "I'm making a herb tea. If you drink it every day, it should settle your stomach."

Cody tentatively touched the plant in its damp tissue. "I never thought about it before. If everyone just took care of their own little patch of dirt, the Earth would be OK, wouldn't it?"

I saw the aunts exchange glances behind her back. Aunt Bonita said gruffly, "It'd be a start."

CHAPTER FIFTEEN

I'd never seen Cody so happy as she was on that walk. When Earl Brokeshoulder rang to say he'd found her a suitable pony, she looked like she'd died and gone to Heaven!

"Not to be a party pooper, but I'm waiting for the big meltdown," I told Helix. It came sooner than I thought.

Later that afternoon, stretching to get something off the shelf for Aunt Jeannie, Cody knocked an old-fashioned sweetie tin to the floor. The lid wasn't put back properly and bags of tiny beads instantly emptied themselves all over the trailer. Cody looked at the hundreds of beads rolling everywhere and an old memory exploded from her mind to mine.

A little dark-haired girl in denim overalls, carefully

picking up tiny beads between her finger and thumb, naming the colours in English, "Black, yellow, red." Then she named them in her daddy's language. "*Lzhini, litsoof, lichii...*"

Julia saw what she was doing. Her face went rigid. "Don't let her play with those, Bonita," she said sharply. "She might choke."

"She's fine. I'm watching her," said a younger, mellower Aunt Bonita. "She's learning her daddy's language, aren't you, clever girl?"

"Are you deaf! I said *no!*" Julia lunged at her daughter. Suddenly beads were flying everywhere and little Cody howled. In her two-year-old's mind the spilled beads seemed somehow mixed up with the confusing adult emotions that were suddenly let loose in the room.

Back in the present, Cody collapsed in a storm of weeping. I was upset for her, also shocked. Cody had suffered more than any teenage girl should have to, but I'd never seen her shed a single tear until now. Aunt Bonita's eyes went dark with sorrow, but she didn't move to comfort her, just nodded tightly to herself. She seemed to guess what had triggered this outburst of grief.

I put my arms invisibly around Cody, murmuring soothing words. I don't even know what. I could feel her raw emotions like jagged slices of glass. It was like long ago something inside Cody got broken and she'd only just now felt the pain.

Cody was still putting the beads into their proper compartments when Jim Yellowbird arrived to pick up the truck.

"You're doing a good job there," he told her. "You planning to do some Navajo beadwork while you're here?"

Cody ducked her head, not wanting this kind old man to see she'd been crying. "They got mixed up," she mumbled. "I'm just putting them away."

"My wife used to do beadwork. All the women in her family did. Next time I'm over I'll bring some of her work. You might be interested." Jim's eyes twinkled. "Of course no one has the patience now. They're all on – what's it called? – Instant Messenger! Bet you're one of them e-mail females too?"

Cody managed a watery smile. "I guess."

"So how're you settling into Ghost Canyon?" he asked her. "You're probably missing your friends, am I right?"

"Not really..." she started.

Jim Yellowbird yelled through to the kitchen. "Hey, Bonita! You want to get Cody enrolled at the local high school. She doesn't want to mope around here all day long."

"But I like it here," Cody protested. She sounded panicky. "I won't be here long enough to go to school. Mom will be out of hospital in a couple of weeks, and I'll have to go back."

"That's a real shame. It's a good school." Jim shifted position on the couch, removed a bead from under his behind and handed it solemnly to Cody. "Mind you," he admitted, "I still get chills every time I go through those gates. How about you, Bonita?"

Aunt Bonita came in with the coffee pot. "Just remembering our school days gives me the chills, " she said with feeling. "A lot of us were sent to government-run boarding schools," she explained to Cody.

"Did they send you?" Cody asked her.

Aunt Bonita poured Jim a cup of strong black coffee. "Me and all my sisters."

"I bawled my eyes out every night that first year," Jim remembered. "Navajo boys aren't supposed to cry," he explained ruefully to Cody, "and there I was, sobbing like a little girl." He shook his head. "You know we were forbidden to talk our own language? If they caught us talking in Navajo the teachers gave us a beating."

Worse than the beatings, according to Jim, was the food. "Cheese sandwiches every single day! When I went home for the holidays my mama said I smelled like a billy goat! All that cheese made my stomach swell up like a dead fish!"

"Navajo kids don't tend to tolerate dairy so well," Aunt Bonita explained to Cody.

She looked up from her beads. "I eat dairy."

"And your belly feels bad all the time, ain't that right?" said her aunt quietly.

"It was my grandmother who saved me," said Jim Yellowbird. "She said I mustn't be ashamed of crying. She said some people take on the pain and suffering for the whole tribe, so others can be brave. After that it didn't feel so bad."

I saw Cody absorbing this information. "Did she really mean that?" she asked a little shyly.

Aunt Bonita lightly passed her hand over Cody's head in its knitted beanie. It was the first openly loving gesture I'd seen her make to her great niece. "Jim's grandma was a wise woman. Some people, like your mom, seem to carry the whole world's pain inside their bellies. You're that way yourself, Cody."

Cody went quiet. I don't think anyone had ever talked about her mum's illness in that way. Instead of something shameful, Aunt Bonita made it sound like a painful kind of gift.

That evening Roxie dropped off little Tazbah for the night

so she could go out dancing with her boyfriend Dwayne. I never quite figured out what relation Roxie was to the aunts, but you could tell Tazbah stayed with them a LOT. She waved a cheery bye-bye to her mum, and was soon building card houses with Cody. When she got tired, Aunt Jeannie rocked her, singing an old Navajo lullaby.

Cody abruptly vanished into her room, dragging her curtain across for privacy. I found her sitting on her bed, rocking herself in her own arms. Tears trickled down her cheeks.

"Do you think she remembers the lullaby?" I whispered to Helix.

Yes and it hurts, Helix beamed back. *Martin sang that same lullaby the night before her mum took her away from Arizona. They were the last Navajo words Cody heard spoken – until you brought her back to the Rez.*

"The aunts brought her back, not me," I objected. "The aunts and Ambriel. I just tagged along."

Rubbish! said Helix briskly. *The Universe brought you and Cody together for a v. important reason, so important it's setting off major alarm bells in the Hell dimensions as we speak.*

"Seriously?"

The Dark Powers can see all their work going up in smoke. They're not happy about it. Be on your guard, sweetie, OK? Her warning left me on edge.

After Cody was asleep I sat up listening to my iPod, using just one of the little ear-buds, leaving the other ear free in case something kicked off.

I was listening to "Melanie's Song" (Version Two), idly scrolling through my iPod menu. I felt a pang as I came across a home movie Lola shot months ago, a montage of me and Reubs kidding around on a boat trip on one of the Heavenly canals. It upset me too much to watch. I paused the movie on Reuben's laughing face.

Where ARE you, angel boy? I wondered helplessly. I'd had a text from Lola telling me they'd arrived safely, that they'd be out searching every day, and she'd let me know when there was any news. After that, nothing.

Suddenly something didn't feel right. I whipped out my ear-bud, and the night suddenly erupted with furious yips and howls. Something was freaking the dogs.

Next minute I was flying to the front door. I charged out into the darkness yelling every battle cry I'd ever learned in angelic history at the top of my voice. The hideous creature in front of me reared up on its hind legs in surprise like a bear. Hairless as a monstrous worm, its skin glowed with a sickly green light.

For an instant our eyes met in mutual loathing, then it dropped on to all fours, baring its pointed teeth in a snarl of fury. Then it loped off with the aunts' dogs hurtling after it.

Behind me I heard Aunt Bonita come stumbling out of her room. She flung open the door, screaming in Navajo. "Get away from here, you Death Eater! This time she's staying!"

Her oldest, fiercest dog, an elderly bulldog cross, was the first to disappear into the trees snarling its own ferocious battle cry. I heard a harrowing scream and knew I was listening to that brave dog's death throes.

I was shaking. I was desperate to delete the creature's disgusting image from my memory bank, but it had burned itself into my brain.

Aunt Bonita disappeared back into the trailer. I assumed she'd gone to check on Tazbah. Then I smelled scorching herbs and Cody's aunt appeared with a smouldering branch of sage brush. She hobbled outside in her flowery, old lady PJs and started swirling the cleansing smoke around her home, north, south, east and west, purifying her trailer of the evil vibes. Then she grabbed a torch and went to find her dog.

It seemed like a long time before I heard her return, staggering slightly under its weight. The dog was already turning stiff in her arms. I heard her talking to it with rough affection. "You died a good death protecting Martin's daughter. This Earth walk is finished for you. Now your spirit can run free in the canyon."

I sat outside the trailer for the rest of the night. I

didn't think the creature would be back in a hurry, but an angel on your front step never hurts.

Tazbah woke up at first light, singing, "Morning's here! Morning's here!" Roxie's little girl seemed to think the sunrise had been arranged totally for her benefit!

Careful not to wake Cody, Aunt Bonita got Tazbah dressed and fed, then she called Aunt Evalina on the phone. "Get over here right away and bring Jeannie," she told her in a low voice. Minutes later the old ladies softly let themselves in, still in their nightclothes.

"It killed one of my dogs," Aunt Bonita told them in an undertone. "I burned sage, but sage won't keep that one away for long I'm gonna call Earl, ask him if he'll drop Cody off at the school. We'll be back before school's out."

"Where are we going?" asked Aunt Jeannie.

Aunt Evalina already knew. "We're going to see Butterfly Woman."

Chapter Sixteen

An hour later the aunts were buttoning coats over bunchy Navajo skirts and Cody was whingeing about having to spend her day in school. "Why can't I come see her too?" She knew they were hiding something from her and it made her act like a cranky little kid. "How will you even get there?" she asked, thinking up new objections. "Jim Yellowbird took the truck."

"Walk," said Aunt Bonita crisply. "It's less than sixty minutes to Butterfly Woman's house if you walk fast."

"That's not her *actual* name, right, 'Butterfly Woman'?" Cody said it like it was the stupidest name she'D ever heard.

"Trust me!" I warned her. "Butterfly Woman is her real name!" Even *I* got goosebumps every time I heard it. I didn't need anyone to tell me she was a woman of power.

"Butterfly Woman is nearly a hundred years old; her name is her own business," Aunt Bonita snapped.

"Earl's here," Aunt Evalina told Cody.

Cody stomped out to the waiting patrol car. Earl took one look and said humorously, "Oh, it's like that!" She hunched her shoulders, ignoring the aunts' waves as the car bumped off down the track.

Earl just let her be. After a while she complained, "I just don't get why they had to go rushing off to see this Butterfly person. They never said last night. Oh, don't tell me," she added grumpily. "It's 'the Navajo way'!"

Earl spread his hands. "I ain't saying a word while you're in this mood. I might get my head snapped off!"

They drove in silence for a while then Cody snorted, "Admit it, I am going to have the worst day. What do you bet Lily's going to introduce me to the kids as a lost bird?"

He shook his head. "I doubt it. When I saw her yesterday she was a bag of nerves. This is a big day for Lily. The school's holding its first ever Grandparents' Day. Lily's been organising it for months. She's terrified no one will turn up."

"Why wouldn't they?" asked Cody.

"Some of the old-timers on the Rez didn't have such

good school experiences. Lily's hoping to show them that's all changed and modern Navajo schools can be welcoming, friendly places." He glanced across at Cody. "I know Lily can be a bit intense, but her heart's in the right place."

When Lily saw Cody hovering awkwardly at the back of the school hall she almost cried with relief. "Cody, what a sight for sore eyes! We are desperate for another pair of hands!"

The hall was full of overexcited little kids running around in their underwear. Some of the older kids were helping them into their costumes, others were frantically practising either their lines or their dance steps. The air was practically pulsing with stage fright.

For a moment Cody looked like she wanted to run, then she took a breath. "Tell me what to do." And next minute she was helping a little boy called Toby Manybeads into a pair of home-made eagle's wings.

Lily had been right to worry as it turned out. Cody helped her set out two hundred chairs, but less than twenty grandparents showed up for her big day. Those who made the effort, though, obviously had a ball.

First the younger kids put on their musical show, starting with a funky Navajo version of "Mary Had a Little Lamb". Lily Topaha had written Navajo-type lyrics about Grandpa planting corn, the baby in its cradleboard,

Grandma weaving a rug under a tree etc. The excitement was too much for one little girl who simply stopped singing, walked offstage, climbed up on to Cody's lap and serenely went to sleep. I saw Cody softly stroke her shiny hair, the exact colour of Cody's own.

Later the grandparents took over the school kitchen to prepare a traditional Navajo meal. A photographer from one of the reservation newspapers snuck around snapping photos of the tribal elders sternly instructing their grandkids in the right way to make Navajo frybread.

Finally, the older kids did a presentation of the Navajo Creation story in song and dance. This is basically the story:

Long ago all of Earth's creatures lived in the Black World. No one was happy, so they decided to leave. They travelled from world to world, but none of them seemed right until finally they entered the Glittering World, a beautiful place where everything was in perfect balance, and animals, humans and spirits could live in harmony.

The Glittering World, I whispered then quickly glanced around. Was it just my imagination or did I feel a sighing, golden breath? Though I couldn't see him, I had the strangest feeling Ambriel had been watching as the children sang and danced their way through his dream.

After the performance the teachers invited all the grandparents back to their classrooms to view the children's artwork. The walls of Lily's classroom glowed with brightly coloured paintings depicting Navajo myths and legends. I saw several paintings of Coyote impatiently hurling the stars up into the sky. One girl had painted a picture of Spider Woman weaving the world together with her rainbow-coloured threads.

Toby's grandpa chatted to Cody as they both admired Toby's painting of Red Jacket. "He's like the Navajo Santa Claus. Except his sleigh is pulled through the sky by magic buffalo, not reindeer!"

I saw Toby tug on Cody's hand. "I did another painting. It's scary though," he added doubtfully.

If you hadn't seen one yourself in real life, the creature in Toby's painting might seem comical, a six-year-old's idea of a monster, baring pointed teeth. The colour drained from Cody's face. "I've – I've got to get some air." She went rushing out.

I saw Grandpa Manybeads shake his head in disapproval. "These are not things to put on display in school." He unpinned the picture and stuffed it in his pocket, but not before I'd seen the title in Toby's six-year-old scrawl:

The Skin Walker.

What's a Skin Walker? I'd asked and Brice had done a mock shudder. *You don't want to know.*

More than the actual picture of the Skin Walker it was Cody's reaction that disturbed me. Why was she so freaked? She'd been asleep the night the creature came sniffing around. Where had she seen one? And *when*?

On the drive back Earl put in a CD. Soon he was nodding his head to the beat. He saw Cody's amazed expression and laughed. "Did you think we just listen to chicken scratch music and *heya heya* chants?"

"No," she said, embarrassed. "I didn't know you had Navajo rappers, that's all."

They listened to the rapper for a few minutes. Cody's eyes kept going back to Earl's driving mirror where something was hanging from a strip of leather. "Is that an actual bear's claw?" she asked at last.

He nodded. "Had that since I was thirteen years old. Got it on my vision fast. On the fourth day a bear came into my camp. He took my medicine pouch and left me this claw."

Cody gasped. "Weren't you scared!"

"Awed more than scared. Strange things happen on a vision fast, but somehow in your inner world they make total sense."

"So what's it like when you get a vision?" Cody was fascinated. "Is it like, truly amazing?"

He smiled at her enthusiasm. "It's different for everyone. Sometimes you get a new name, a name you will carry through your adult life. Sometimes the Holy People grant you glimpses of the life path they want you to follow."

"Do girls have to do vision fasts?" Cody sounded oddly hopeful.

Earl shook his head. "Girls have their own ceremony called *Kinaalda*. My sister Vickie had hers last year. The only time a Navajo girl goes on a vision fast, that I heard of, is if she gets apprenticed to a traditional healer or herb woman. I don't think that's ever happened in my lifetime."

Cody took a sudden breath. "Can I ask you something? Are you supposed to say Native American or American Indian?"

He shrugged. "Doesn't matter to me. You know why people call us 'Indians', right?"

"Not really."

"OK, so Chris Columbus rocks up to the shores of the New World, and immediately thinks he's found a short cut to India. YEEHAAR! He can't wait to start trading all those desirable Indian spices. His fortune is as good as made!"

"Except it wasn't India," said Cody, giggling.

"True, but hey, to Chris we're all funny brown

foreigners, right! Eventually our hero found out his mistake, but the name stuck. Butterfly Woman says that from the start white people never really saw us; they always saw what they expected to see."

Earl smiled at Cody. "People like Lily who are, you know, real *earnest* about their roots, believe we shouldn't be stuck with a name that only came about because of some stupid mix-up. I say it's ALL a stupid mix-up. Why is it better to call us 'Native Americans'? America is their name for this country, not ours."

Cody looked out of the window. "Aunt Bonita says all I know is white people's history."

Earl sighed. "Cody, some days all that skin colour talk makes me come over real tired. On those days I'd rather go hang out with the bears." His eyes glinted with humour. "Any colour bears!"

A burst of static came over Earl's radio, something about a bar fight. "Marlon can get that one," he said cheerfully. "Look, I've got Saturday off. Why don't I bring my sister over and we'll show you the sights?"

Cody looked wary. "Was she one of the girls at the party?"

He laughed. "If you have to ask, Vickie *definitely* wasn't there!"

That night the aunts lined up on the couch to watch a

TV programme about Miss Navajo. "Another couple of years and we can enter Cody," Aunt Jeannie teased. "Reckon you could butcher a sheep, Cody?"

Cody looked revolted. "Miss Navajo has to kill a *sheep*?"

"Of course!" Aunt Evalina seemed to be enjoying the joke. "Navajo girls have to be useful not just cute to look at!" Cody's aunts were at it again, exchanging sly nods and glances over their niece's head. I could feel them leading up to something.

"We were talking to Butterfly Woman," Aunt Bonita said super-casually. "She thinks while you're here you should do your *Kinaalda* ceremony. She thinks it would help you."

"Help me how?" Cody was suddenly suspicious.

"Help you become stronger inside," Aunt Evalina said. "After your *Kinaalda* you will always be a part of us. No matter where you go, you can still draw strength from the tribe. That's what Butterfly Woman said."

Cody looked wary. "Does a *Kinaalda* involve sheep at all?"

Aunt Evalina laughed. "No! You have to run though! Can you run?"

"Hey, I'm a Navajo girl," Cody said, surprising everyone including herself. "Obviously I run like the wind!"

"So will you do it?" Aunt Bonita made it sound like she didn't care either way.

Cody thought for a minute. "OK!" The aunts beamed with relief. They hadn't thought she'd agree.

"We'll start organising it right away," Aunt Jeannie promised.

My phone had been silent for days so it was a shock to feel it suddenly vibrating inside my jacket. I fumbled with the buttons.

"Lola! You found him, right!" The signal was bad, making her voice drift in and out as if she was floating in deep space, but I could hear Lola was crying.

"Absolutely no sign. Mel, I'm so sorry. I just thought you should know." We both cried for a while then Lola pulled herself together.

"We've been everywhere. In every cave, behind every waterfall. We've been in every monastery, every mountain inn. Brice dragged us into one today that was basically just someone's front room. They heated it with a tiny stove that burned yak dung. The lamps burned yak butter so everything *reeked* of yak. Brice made us stay there for *hours*. He said he had a hunch we'd overhear something useful.

I gave a hysterical giggle. It was the kind of mad thing Brice would do. "Did you? Hear anything useful?" I asked hopefully, though I already knew the answer.

"No, but it was interesting," Lola admitted. "One old guy told a story about something that happened years ago when he was out hunting on the mountains. He was hot on the trail of a snow leopard when a scary sorcerer with yellow eyes appeared and warned him to stop. He said without the snow leopards the valley would die. The guy never hunted leopards again."

Snow leopards and sorcerers. It sounded like another world.

After I rang off, I wiped my eyes and dug my notebook out of my bag. I couldn't help my friends search for Reuben, but I could do what Reubs would do if he was here with me now. I could do my job to the best of my ability, giving Cody five-star cosmic protection.

She'd gone to bed by this time. I softly leaned over her to check that she was sleeping soundly, then I perched beside her with my notebook, thoughtfully chewing the end of my pen. I needed answers, but what I'd got was a bigger, more confusing riddle.

Eventually I scribbled:

Butterfly Woman – what's so special about her? Find out more.

After a long pause I scrawled underneath:

What the sassafras is a skin walker?

Suddenly I was fumbling for my phone. "Lola, is Brice with you?"

"Sure," she said in surprise. "I'll put him on."

"Hi, sweetheart," said a familiar voice. "How's life on the Rez?"

"I need you to tell me everything you know about Skin Walkers," I told him.

I heard Lola's boyfriend inhale sharply. "Do you think you've seen one?"

"That's what I need to find out."

I sat in total silence as Brice shared the results of his research, then I thanked him and rang off. I went back to chewing my pen for a minute, then I picked up my spangly new phone and carefully typed *Skin Walker* into the search engine.

Thanks to Brice, I was ninety-nine per cent convinced that what I'd seen was *not* a bona fide Skin Walker, but I needed to make sure. Plus, to be totally honest, I needed to keep busy. While I was checking cosmic info, I was just a brain, a pair of eyes scanning tiny print. Turning back into an angel girl would mean having to face that waiting wall of worry and grief. I jumped from link to link, reading what the celestial websites had to say and learned some v. disturbing things.

I already knew from Brice that Navajo people associate Skin Walkers with witches. According to the websites, a Navajo witch is basically just a twisted human who follows the Evil Way instead of the Blessing Way. To get their evil powers, the witches must perform a v.v. Dark act which we don't need to go into here. Even in the twenty-first century, many Navajo still believed that a witch had the power to send out a part of themselves in the shape of a hideous beast, aka a Skin Walker.

Brice said this kind of belief was pure gold to the PODS. "At the end of the day, darling, it doesn't matter if they exist or not. The PODS can mimic any form they like. If the locals believe in fire-breathing demons, they'll assume the form of a fire-breathing demon. If they believe in Skin Walkers..."

I read on, shivering, glad of the shimmery light coming from my phone, until I found a paragraph that almost made my hair stand on end.

"Witches often send Skin Walkers to steal hair or anything closely connected with their chosen victim. That's why the Navajo only allow relatives such as mothers and wives to cut their hair and even then they burn or bury it..."

I remembered Cody flushing her hair down the toilet in a panic. *She knew something was after her, like she knew about Skin Walkers. Without being told, she knew.*

Mr Allbright likes to joke that missions are like angel cake. He means they both have like, *layers*.

On the surface Cody's return to the reservation was

a huge success. A lot of people genuinely seemed to care about her. Jim Yellowbird dropped by, bringing samples of his late wife's beadwork as he'd promised. He sat on the front porch explaining all the tiny patterns to Cody and what they meant.

"It's like a story in beads!" she said, amazed.

Before he left, Jim gave her a beaded pouch with the design of a turtle. "Might inspire you to do your own beadwork." He gave one of his sly grins. "Do it between e-mails!"

The same evening Earl drove over in his own beat-up truck with a horsebox attached. Cody and the aunts helped to lead the pony out of the box. He looked exactly like Indian ponies you see in movies, a magical speckled mix of browns and golds. The horse swivelled calm brown eyes to look at me, snickering a greeting.

"You beauty. You are *exactly* what Cody needs," I told him.

"Meet Pepper," Earl said, smiling. "Think you two can get along?" Cody was too completely overcome to speak.

Mr Allbright says the hardest thing on a v. complicated mission is that you want to believe the pretty, sugary top layer is all there is, and it's true. I didn't want to know about those ominous layers twanging underneath. But even as Cody let Pepper nuzzle her cheek, they were there.

"See how quickly she's got his trust," Aunt Evalina whispered to her sisters. "That child is Navajo to her bones."

"Not according to some people," said Aunt Bonita grimly. "I was in Basha's this morning, checking out the special offers, and I heard one of Dolores Bitterwater's cronies running her mouth."

Aunt Evalina nodded unhappily. "Nettie told me what Dolores has been saying."

"What's she been saying?" Aunt Jeannie was bewildered.

"Remember the night that *thing* came slinking round?" Aunt Evalina said in a low voice. "Dolores' husband just *happened* to be taking a short cut through our place, coming back late from a party. Now they're spreading rumours that Cody is a *chiindi*."

"Just happened to be up to no good, more like!" I'd never seen Aunt Jeannie so angry. "Nobody in their right mind could think that about Cody!"

Aunt Bonita covered her face with her bony hands. "I thought we had more time. I thought once she had her *Kinaalda* people would accept her as one of us..."

I was already scribbling furiously in my notebook,

but I actually didn't need to look it up. I was almost sure I knew what *chiindi* meant.

Like hysterical American colonists in sixteenth-century Salem, people in Ghost Canyon were accusing Cody of being a witch.

CHAPTER SEVENTEEN

Next day, after school, Cody and I went riding out into the canyon with Lily Topaha.

It was a hazy, golden afternoon, the hottest day of the year so far. Lily said the spring never lasted long in Arizona.

"These will be gone in a blink." She gestured at the tiny wild flowers scattered as far as you could see. "Isn't that the most beautiful sight?"

"I love it," Cody admitted. "How my mom talks about it, it always sounded so harsh and scary."

"It can be," Lily warned. "Wait till we get one of our famous Arizona storms!"

They rode for a while in friendly silence. You could tell Cody had warmed to Lily since their first meeting. After a while she said tentatively, "Did you mean it, what you said that night? Were you really stolen as a little baby?"

Lily nodded. "But I wasn't a little baby. I was two years old. My mom and dad were living on welfare. Like a lot of our people in those days we didn't always get enough to eat. Mom was worried I was too thin, so she took me to the clinic. They said I was very sick and they'd have to rush me to hospital right away. They told my parents not to visit. It would just upset me. But when two weeks went by without a word from the hospital, my mom knew something wasn't right. We didn't own a car, so she walked the twelve miles to the hospital and insisted on seeing me, but they said I'd gone. I'd been taken away for adoption."

"That's that's just unbelievable." Cody's voice was shaky.

"It was a lie about me being adopted. I'd been sold," Lily said. "The couple who bought me were Italian Americans. They were desperate for a child, and I guess I looked like I could almost be Italian." She pulled a face. "Unfortunately I developed a few behavioural problems."

"Hello!" said Cody angrily. "What did they *expect!*"

"After eighteen months of the toddler from hell they decided I wasn't their dream coffee-coloured cutie after all and put me in a home." After that Lily said she went to a string of foster homes, so many she lost count.

"How come you're so, you know, *normal*?" asked Cody. "I was in a home for *one* night and I felt like, totally abandoned."

"My mama," Lily said quietly. "She came to me in dreams every night. I couldn't remember her face, even in dreams, but I remembered her hands, cooking, weaving, shucking corn, and I knew her voice. Every night I heard her voice saying she loved me."

Cody swallowed so hard I could literally feel the ache in her throat. "I wish I remembered my dad," she said huskily. "I kind of remember his boots – I *think*. He'd stand me on top of his big leather boots – I think they had wavy patterns on – and we'd dance."

They had stopped at a shallow creek, really just a trickle, to let the horses drink. "How did you find your family again after so long?" Cody seemed genuinely shaken by Lily's story.

Lily laughed. "The Internet, believe it or not! I miraculously graduated from high school, despite all my hang-ups, and while I was at college I started posting messages on Navajo websites."

Lily said one day she was routinely checking the missing persons websites and found a message from Ann-Marie Topaha saying she thought Lily might be her long-lost sister. Their parents had died years before, but there were three brothers, two more sisters and an entire army of uncles, aunts and cousins.

"Wasn't it weird seeing them all after so many years?"

"Weird, wonderful and completely overwhelming," Lily admitted. "The Topahas are a bit intense, as you might have noticed!"

"I don't think that now," Cody said shyly. "You're quite cool actually, now I know you."

That night I scrunched myself into Cody's little wicker chair and tried my best to catch a few Zs. It was no go from the start. There were some REALLY unsettling energies swirling around the canyon.

I briefly went out to take a look and saw a huge full moon riding high above the trailer. Angels are sensitive to these kinds of cosmic influences. The spangly silver moonlight wouldn't be helping my sleep problem one bit.

Luckily I'd brought the cunning eye mask Lola gave me for missions. It seemed to help. I was almost dozing when I found myself unexpectedly splitting into two: the v. tired angel girl in Cody's chair and a shimmery second self who floated gently out into the desert.

I was like, *Woo! What's going on?*

Then I saw the ghosts. I couldn't even guess at how

many there were – thousands and thousands, an endless column winding away into the distance. Over the slow shuffle of moccasins and the desolate cries of babies, I could hear angry yells as soldiers in old-style uniforms rode up and down like cowboys controlling cattle, forcing them to keep moving.

As each ghostly man or woman passed, they turned to look at me, so that I saw each face with dreamlike clarity: a bewildered old man; an exhausted mother with another baby on the way, carrying a shocked, bloodstained toddler on her back; a long-haired warrior bleeding from a neck wound. Behind the warrior walked a dignified little girl whose face was so familiar I almost shouted with surprise. She looked back at me with Cody's solemn dark eyes, as if she needed me to understand something.

"I'll take care of her," I whispered. "I promise." Then I was just one angel girl again, curled up in the small wicker chair in Cody's room.

"You look like roadkill!" Aunt Bonita told Cody bluntly next morning. "Sure you're up to a day out?"

"I'll be fine," Cody said, avoiding her eyes. "I'm tired, that's all."

Earl and Vickie Brokeshoulder both got out of the car as Cody came shyly out to join them. I hardly recognised Earl out of uniform. Earl's sister was dressed like a typical American teen in denim jeans and T-shirt, apart from her beaded Navajo earrings.

"My brother wants you to sit up front. He says I keep bugging him!" Vickie told Cody with a grin.

"I'd wear my hair short like yours if I didn't have a big nose," she added as the car jolted down the track.

"You don't have a big nose!" said Cody in surprise.

"Sure she does," Earl said with a grin. "She has the Brokeshoulder nose, don't you, sis?"

Then Earl's sister dropped a bombshell. "You do know your boots are the talk of Ghost Canyon?" she asked matter of factly.

Cody looked dismayed. "You're kidding. Why?"

Earl gave Vickie a look, but Vickie wasn't a girl you could easily silence. "Navajo people have big issues about death," she explained calmly. "Some people think anyone who deliberately puts a death symbol on their clothes must automatically be a witch."

Cody looked as if she didn't know whether to laugh or cry. "People think I'm a WITCH! Why didn't the aunts *tell* me?"

Vickie shrugged. "I guess they didn't want to upset you."

"They didn't want— but Aunt Bonita upsets people all the *time*!"

"Cody, I don't think you realise," Vickie said earnestly. "Having you here after all these years – it's huge for them. They want you to feel like you belong, that you're part of our lives."

Cody was still in shock. "They still should have said." She glanced at Vickie, seemed to hesitate, then said awkwardly, "When I painted the skulls, it was, you know, quite a bad time in my life."

Vickie flashed her a grin. "Hey, I should paint some skulls on mine! We'll tell Dolores we're starting a cult!"

Earl rolled his eyes. "Yeah, Vickie, that'll smooth things over!"

Having got the skulls out of the way, the girls chatted like they'd known each other all their lives. Vickie described herself as a total nerd. "It's sad, but I love studying!" They moved on to music, how the tunes on their iPods were like their diaries, a totally faithful record of their current state of mind. They discussed fave ice cream (they both rated Ben & Jerry's Brownie Chocolate Chip). Then Vickie asked Cody for her first impressions of the reservation.

"I thought it looked like a total junkheap," Cody said frankly, then turned bright red. "Sorry, that came out sounding really offensive."

Vickie shook her head. "No, it's true. But did you ever think about the rubbish you guys surround yourselves with? Ugly buildings that blot out the light, cars that pollute the air, oil spillages killing the oceans."

Plastic bags, I thought, remembering the dying birds.

Cody frowned. "Like, white people are obsessed with having super-tidy homes and gardens, but they don't mind messing up the planet for future generations?"

"I just think we should *all* clean up our act," Vickie said calmly.

For a while both girls looked out at the scenery. Above us a small town literally clung to the side of the canyon. The teeny doll's houses were painted happy pastel colours, making me think of confetti at a wedding.

Earl gave Vickie a sly look. "Has Bobby forgiven you yet?"

"Excuse *me*, I should be forgiving *him*!" objected Vickie.

"Bobby Blackhorse patted my little sister's tail feathers in the cafeteria," Earl explained.

Vickie giggled. "I emptied a jug of water over him. That cooled him down!"

Cody gasped. "The whole jug!"

"Every last little drop," she said with satisfaction. I snickered. I was liking Vickie more by the minute.

"It was all over Ghost Canyon by nightfall," said Earl.

Cody's smile faded. "I thought Ghost Canyon was

just like some random name at first, but it's really haunted, isn't it?"

"Why wouldn't it be? The entire reservation is built on our people's bones." Earl sounded unusually edgy.

"Shut up, Earl," Vickie said irritably. "I want to hear what happened to Cody."

Cody didn't seem sure if she should tell them. "It's just – I had this weird dream. Actually I'm not sure if it was really a dream. I was standing out in the desert. Another girl was with me, about my age. There was so much light around her I couldn't see her face properly, but she wore similar style clothes to me. Hers were really bright colours though, and her boots had painted butterflies instead of skulls."

I almost shrieked. I could *not* believe Cody had seen me in her dream. It was like, in some strange, mystical space between dreams and real life, we'd genuinely connected. Cody went on to describe her dream – basically everything I'd seen down to the little Navajo girl who looked like Cody.

Earl seemed shaken. "I think that little girl was your ancestor, the ancestor who sent you that dream. She showed you the Long Walk."

"We learned about that in school," Vickie shuddered. "The soldiers shot at everyone who refused to leave. People said the shooting went on all one afternoon. They said the gunfire was so intense it sounded like frying." She swallowed. "By the time they finished, the cliffs were running red with blood."

"Don't!" Cody turned to stare out of the window. This part of the canyon was filled with pure peach orchards. Birds sang. Bees buzzed in the blossom. It was the most peaceful place imaginable, if you didn't know any Navajo history.

Cody said abruptly, "Does everybody here hate white people?"

Vickie looked shocked. "Cody! What a thing to say!"

"I would if I were you," she said in a choked voice. "I'm half white and when I'm listening to all these stories, I hate myself."

"Don't," said Earl firmly. "You got born into a real confused world, Cody, that's all. It's good to know where you come from, but try not to get stuck there, OK?"

"Stop, stop!" Cody's face was white. Earl and Vickie looked bewildered. "I mean it – stop the car!"

Earl braked with a screech of rubber and Cody jumped out.

Someone had abandoned a sack of rubbish at the side of the road. Cody swiftly untied the knot in the neck of the sack. One after another she pulled out three limp furry bodies. Vickie ran to join her. They looked down at the dead puppies in dismay.

Cody reached into the sack one more time without much hope and dragged out a fourth. She gasped. "This one's breathing!"

Vickie quickly glanced about them, getting her bearings. "We'll take him to Butterfly Woman. She's just a few miles from here." Cody scooped up the puppy and they ran back to the car.

"Change of plan," Vickie told her brother. "We're going to Butterfly Woman. Earl, it's *dying*. DRIVE!"

Bad stuff happens; we all know that. Puppies die. Even angels can't save them all. Yet as Earl stepped on the gas, I had a sudden cosmic flash. I knew this puppy was *supposed* to survive. Cody and I must have shared the same flash. She'd gone running to its rescue before she knew what she'd find in the sack.

I watched the puppy's bony little ribs rise and fall as it gasped for oxygen, then I put my hands softly over its chest, beaming the gentle vibes Mr Allbright thinks are suitable for baby animals. Next minute Cody silently placed her hands over mine.

I looked down in surprise at her stubby human fingers with their bitten nails and my shimmery angel fingers eerily occupying the same space. A sudden shocking flood of heat flowed through our joined hands.

Cody hadn't heard about the rules for healing baby animals. She just pulled on some invisible energy supply and *whoosh!* I saw rainbow colours come streaming back into the puppy's aura. It opened its eyes and feebly wagged its ridiculously teeny-tiny tail. We all looked at Cody, amazed.

Earl gave a low whistle. "Well, well, Ms Fortuna. Exactly how long were you planning to keep those superpowers under wraps?"

"I don't have superpowers," Cody said, going red. She didn't want to think she'd done anything unusual.

"Your new best friend disagrees!" Vickie was watching the puppy gratefully lick Cody's hand, making soft puppy whimpers.

My mind flashed back to Julia at Thanksgiving: *Could you put your hands on my head? It sometimes feels better when you put your hands on my head.*

I'd known Cody was special, even without Sam's hints. But I had never dreamed she was a healer, a fabulously gifted healer at that. With eighty per cent of her life force still locked inside her energy system, she had managed to bring a dying puppy back to life. *Imagine if she freed up that eighty per cent*, I thought.

All that healing energy flying around had brought Helix online. *That answers one question in your notebook, hon*, she pointed out. *Why Cody Fortuna is on the PODS' hit list. With a gift like that, she's a major threat.*

"Just what I was thinking," I told her.

And they won't stop, Helix warned. *Cody's waking up, she's starting to use her gifts. They're going to make a move, sweetie, I can feel it. They're going to try to stop her once and for all.*

Cody was gazing down at the puppy with such a soft, open expression, I suddenly felt deeply afraid. Helix was right. Cody was in more danger now than she'd ever been in her life.

"Still want me to drive to Butterfly Woman?" asked Earl.

Vickie nodded. "Scooter's just had puppies. She might let this little guy nurse. Stop off at Basha's first so I can buy tobacco."

"You *smoke*?" said Cody disapprovingly.

Vickie laughed. "Butterfly Woman uses it in her ceremonies. In our culture it's considered rude for a guest to arrive empty-handed!"

"So is she like, a medicine woman or whatever?" Cody asked in a whisper as they walked up the track to Butterfly Woman's *hogan*.

"She's a traditional healer, star gazer, chanter, dream walker. There aren't many of her kind left. When she—" Earl stopped what he was going to say, obviously troubled.

When we walked in, Butterfly Woman was sitting up

in a straight-backed wooden chair. A Navajo blanket in a vibey woven pattern of red and blue diamonds was draped over her shoulders. A much younger woman crouched at a small wood stove, boiling water for tea.

You know those maps of major rivers? Butterfly Woman's lined, wrinkled face was like that. She had the brightest eyes I'd ever seen. Her *hogan* had just the basics: two chairs, a wood stove, a shelf with pans, cups, plates. This simple, almost empty house had that vibe of deep stillness you feel just before morning comes.

The moment I walked in, I knew Butterfly Woman didn't have long to live, a year at most. I could tell she knew this and was totally accepting, enjoying the time she had left, interested in whatever the Universe brought to her door, even a tiny puppy no one wanted.

She inspected the pup all over and gave a creaky old lady's laugh. "A coyote got in with their pooch," she announced in Navajo. "That's why they didn't want him." Vickie translated for Cody.

"I don't care if those puppies were half mongoose," Cody said fiercely. "They shouldn't have dumped them in a sack."

"He was dying," Vickie told Butterfly Woman in Navajo. "Cody brought him back."

Butterfly Woman turned those disturbingly bright

eyes on Cody. "You brought this little puppy back to life?" Vickie quickly translated. "What did you do?" Butterfly Woman asked with interest.

"I – I went really hot and something made me put my hands on him."

"Done anything like that before?" Butterfly Woman probed.

"A little," Cody admitted. "My mom has these bad spells. If I put my hands on her head it sometimes helps."

"Your mama gets sick a lot, don't she?" Butterfly Woman had a slightly pouncing look. Michael gets that same super-focused look when he's looking into your soul. Cody nodded, swallowing.

"Do you have bad dreams, see things that shouldn't be there?"

Cody's mouth started to tremble. "My mom says it's because I'm under a curse."

Butterfly Woman's eyes flashed with anger. "Who's supposed to have cursed you, child?"

"My dad," Cody whispered.

"That sweet boy, never!" Butterfly Woman gripped the wooden arm of her chair, her gnarled hands suddenly trembling with emotion. "I brought your father up," she said through Vickie. "His mama died and his papa just took off. His sisters had their own families, so Martin came to live with me." She let her eyes linger on

Cody. "Tonya, show her the picture," she said abruptly.

The young woman fetched a small framed photograph, handing it to Cody. Cody stared at it as if she wanted to pull her young handsome father out of the picture and into the room. In his arms a small girl gazed solemnly back at the camera.

My eyes stung with tears. Cody had been right about the boots. The leather had patterns like waves. All these years she'd remembered his boots; she'd remembered dancing with her dad.

"You have lived many rounds as a Navajo," Butterfly Woman told Cody calmly. "But this lifetime is different. This time the Holy People need you to understand life through Anglo and Navajo eyes." She frowned. "People think I heal people. I don't heal anyone. The power of their own minds heals them. I just use herbs and sacred things to bring their mind back into balance and harmony."

"*Hozho*," said Cody impulsively.

Butterfly Woman looked pleased. "*Hozho*. Yes. But you have a new kind of power. I don't understand it, but I see it in your face." Cody started to speak, but Butterfly Woman held up her hand.

"I see evil all around you," she told her sternly. "The Evil Ones tried to destroy your gift. They put wrong thoughts into your poor mother's head. They turned people's minds against you. They gave you the dream that makes you scream in the night. If I could, I would take it away, but you must root it out yourself."

Butterfly Woman gently stroked the puppy as she continued to talk. "You thought so many bad things happened because you yourself were bad and worthless. That wasn't true. It's because you are so precious that the Evil Ones want to harm you."

She fumbled in a pouch at her waist, handing Cody a lump of raw turquoise threaded on a piece of leather. "Sometimes a bad dream gets so close it can seem real. This stone will help you see the truth."

Cody went to give back the photo, but Tonya said, "Butterfly Woman says she was only keeping it for you."

We followed Tonya out to a large shed where Scooter sprawled happily on her side feeding her pups. When Cody showed her the new puppy, Scooter sniffed it over, gave it a quick lick, then gently shifted position to make room.

Cody looked as if she might cry. "She doesn't mind! She doesn't mind that the puppy is half coyote."

"Scooter's a Navajo dog," Earl joked. "She takes care of puppies the Navajo way!"

Watching the puppy cuddle up to Scooter, I understood something for the first time. I understood that huge longing inside Cody. After she split from

Cody's dad, Julia needed her daughter to forget everything to do with her Navajo relatives except the bad parts. To please her fragile mum, that's what Cody did; she forgot.

Lily Topaha survived her life in foster homes because she remembered her mum's hands doing the things Navajo mums do. She heard her voice saying she loved her. Cody just had a fuzzy memory of a pair of boots. Without her Navajo roots, Cody was like the lost piece that makes a jigsaw puzzle totally meaningless. Now she'd been found. Now the puzzle made sense again. Now Cody's energy, the tribe's energy, could start to flow

I was outside the trailor composing my nightly text to Reubs when Lola rang. "No news," she said quickly "Just wanted to know how you are."

I felt something inside me just crumple. "I don't understand how they can just lose an angel," I wept.

"Nor does anybody," she said unhappily. "We can't get a reading on him, we can't get a reading on the leopards. It doesn't make sense, but they're all just – gone."

"The Agency knows when some little bird drops off its perch! How can they *not* know where he is?"

"We *will* find him, Boo. You know that, right?" said Lola fiercely. "We're not going to give up."

"I know!" My voice came out in a wail. "It's just so hard when I'm all by myself."

"I should think it's total agony!" Lola's sympathy totally finished me off. I had to excuse myself for a second to generally get a grip.

"I could never be a permanent GA," I said in a more normal voice when I'd got it back together. "You have to figure everything out on your own. I just keep telling myself, at least you can phone for back-up. Cody doesn't have that option."

"How's she doing?" asked Lola.

"OK, actually. She's loads healthier thanks to Aunt Bonita's herb teas and stuff, plus she's out riding in the canyon every day." I told Lola about Cody healing the puppy and the visit to Butterfly Woman. "That has to be why the PODS needed to separate her from her relations."

"Divide and Rule, Dark Studies 101," Lola sighed.

We said our goodbyes, then Lola remembered, "I forgot to ask, have you seen anything of Ambriel?"

"Not exactly *seen*. I feel him around, watching and wondering."

"Wondering...?"

"What will happen, I guess. He set something in motion, but what happens now is really up to Cody."

"And her guardian angel," Lola reminded me.

"Omigosh, Lola! Cody *saw* me in a dream. She described my boots!" Remembering this gave me goosebumps all over again.

Lola was *so* impressed! "For someone who doesn't rate working alone, you are a genius guardian angel!" she said warmly. "You and Cody must have formed an incredible connection!"

"I don't know, Lollie. You know that angel cake thing Mr Allbright says? There's a layer I'm not seeing and it scares me."

As it turned out I wasn't scared enough. Two days later Aunt Bonita's trailer was struck by lightning.

Chapter Eighteen

Roxie had to go to the hospital for her check-up so Tazbah stayed the night. As usual the little girl woke up singing with the sun. Cody amused her for a while, then took her outside to make friends with Pepper.

I sat on the steps of the trailer, watching Tazbah run about investigating everything with huge excitement. She found a toad sitting by a water butt and settled down on her haunches for a chat. "Hello, Grandpa Toad," she said solemnly. "How you?" The aunts had taught her to greet certain animals, even some trees, like well-respected relatives!

At breakfast Aunt Bonita said her knee was hurting. "A storm's coming," she sighed. "I loved them when I was a girl, but not now. The land's got so dry, the lightest rainfall can turn into a flash flood."

By the time they were clearing away the breakfast dishes, you could see the storm brewing. Huge pillowy clouds rapidly piled up over the canyon and we heard distant growls of thunder. Aunt Bonita said Tazbah should stay indoors so Cody took her off to play a v. limited form of hide-and-seek in her bedroom.

I was going to tag along, but Aunt Jeannie and Aunt Evalina arrived to discuss arrangements for Cody's *Kinaalda*, so I thought I'd stay and listen in. They stopped chatting while Cody wandered back into the sitting room with Roxie's little girl balanced across her hip. At that moment, wearing Butterfly Woman's lump of turquoise around her neck, she looked totally like a Navajo girl. She took a breath and the entire trailer flashed blue-white as lightning tore through her bedroom.

Tazbah screamed with terror. Aunt Evalina ran in with the extinguisher, quickly putting out the fire. There was a blackened hole in the ceiling directly over Cody's bed. The bed where she'd been playing with Tazbah was a charred wreck. If the lightning bolt had struck a few seconds earlier, Cody and Tazbah would both have been killed.

They're going to make a move, sweetie. They're going to try to stop her once and for all. This was the evil Butterfly Woman saw around Cody, the murderous cosmic spite that drove off five guardian angels, leaving her all alone in the Universe.

The aunts were always fabulous in a crisis. They threw essentials into a couple of bags and moved Cody, Tazbah and Aunt Bonita into Aunt Jeannie's trailer. Aunt Jeannie said she'd move in with Aunt Evalina. Aunt Bonita said, assuming the trailer could be repaired, they would have to hold a cleansing ceremony before she and Cody could move back in.

I truly expected Cody to fall apart. I expected her to dredge up the old family story that she'd been cursed, that she destroyed everything she touched. But she just went v. v. quiet.

Tazbah was still howling. Aunt Bonita settled down with her on the couch with her bottle to try to calm her. I sent gentle sleepy vibes, hoping the traumatised little girl might be able to sleep off the shock.

Aunt Evalina brewed a big pot of super-strong coffee, spooning extra sugar into the cups, the aunts' universal remedy. Nobody mentioned being attacked by hostile cosmic forces, but everyone knew that's what had happened.

"I'm going for a walk," Cody said abruptly. I hastily followed her out. I wasn't letting that girl out of my sight after what just happened. To my surprise Cody didn't go anywhere. She just seated herself on a rusty old porch swing, pushing herself back and forth, frowning, deep in thought.

When she went back inside, she had a new stubborn expression. "I don't want to put you guys in danger," she told her aunts, then waved away their protests. "Don't worry, I'm not going to be driven away either! Mom and I were always having to start over. I'm sick to death of starting over. But I'm not like Lily. I'm not a true Navajo."

Aunt Evalina set down her cup. "Cody, you—"

"Please, I need to say this!" Cody said fiercely. "The *Kinaalda* ceremony. Vickie told me about hers, how amazing it was, but—" She hunted for the right words. "I'm really proud of the part of me that's Navajo. If you hadn't brought me back, I never would have known about it. But maybe there are other parts I don't know." She sat down next to Aunt Bonita with little Tazbah between them sucking sleepily at her bottle.

"One day I'll do my *Kinaalda*, if you think I should, but just now I think I need a different kind of ceremony."

Aunt Bonita was scandalised. "You can't just invent your own ceremony! Take a little of this and that like those New Age hippies!"

"I know that. But isn't there something like a vision fast, where kids stay alone in a canyon until the Holy People send a vision?"

"That's not for girls," Aunt Bonita said sharply. "That's when a boy becomes a man."

"What about healers? Don't they go on vision fasts?" Cody's face was glowing with excitement. The aunts looked as if they were suddenly afraid to breathe. "I'm like Butterfly Woman, aren't I?" Cody said.

They gazed at her, amazed. After all their stories, all their bullying and coaxing, Cody had figured it all out for herself.

"Actually I'm *nothing* like Butterfly Woman," Cody corrected herself. "I don't know anything about herbs or dreams or Blessing Way chants – or life, come to that! I've got Butterfly Woman's power, but I still need to learn how to use it."

She sat down next to Tazbah and quite naturally took Aunt Bonita's bony old hand in hers. For a girl who'd narrowly missed being struck by lightning she seemed v.v. together.

"That's why you brought me back, isn't it?" she asked softly. "Butterfly Woman is sick and there's no one to take her place."

"When did you—?" Aunt Bonita broke off. For once she was speechless.

"Will you do it?" Cody begged. "Will you take me where they take the boys? If this is my true home, if the wind really knows my name, like Aunt Evalina says, the Holy People will see I'm serious. They'll send me a vision to show me what I have to do."

The aunts looked at each other. "We can't use the boys' canyon," said Aunt Evalina firmly. "That wouldn't be right."

Aunt Bonita gave her a nudge. "But there's another place..."

Cody gasped. "You'll *let* me?"

Instead of answering, Aunt Bonita just grabbed hold of Cody, hugging her so tightly that little Tazbah, caught in the middle, shrieked in protest.

CHAPTER NINETEEN

To be properly prepared for her vision fast in the wilderness, Cody was sent to live with Butterfly Woman. She stayed there for twenty-eight days, a full lunar month.

A lot of Butterfly Woman's instruction was just practical, teaching her the difference between healing and poisonous plants, how to light a fire with a fire stick. Butterfly Woman also passed on all kinds of sacred knowledge connected to the Blessing Way, things too secret to mention here, and she taught her powerful chants to ward off the Evil Ones.

"When you are weak from hunger and sick from loneliness, then they will come," Butterfly Woman warned her.

During her training period Cody was only permitted to eat v. pure foods. At night she slept on the floor wrapped in a blanket Butterfly Woman herself had woven many years ago. On her final evening Cody was taken into a sweat lodge, a special *hogan* filled with baking hot stones, to be purified body and soul before her encounter with the Holy People.

The aunts arrived on horseback, while it was still dark, Cody's pony Pepper trotting along behind. They helped Cody dress in traditional Navajo clothes: a long skirt and blouse, soft leather boots with embroidered tops. Aunt Evalina placed a necklace of silver squash blossoms around her neck, alongside Butterfly Woman's piece of turquoise, then Aunt Bonita carefully combed out Cody's hair.

"Now you look like a real Navajo girl," she told her.

Cody looked wistful. "Even with my hideous hair?"

"I cut my hair off once," Aunt Jeannie said unexpectedly. "When my husband died. I was so unhappy I wanted to die too, but my children were young and still needed me. I cut my hair because I needed to make a new beginning."

We rode for what seemed like hours until we reached the top of a narrow, wooded canyon.

"We call this Rainbow Canyon. It has been a sacred

place to our people for hundreds of years," Aunt Bonita said. "There's a cave our ancestors used for ceremonies. You might find it if you look."

The aunts were going to be camping close to the top of the canyon. They told Cody to come at noon and leave a pebble for each of the four days of her fast. "That way we'll know you're safe," Aunt Evalina said. They showed her a narrow track, just wide enough for a nimble Navajo pony, then they turned without a word, simply walking away.

Pepper picked his way cautiously down the path where twisty pine trees seemed to grow out of pure rock. At the bottom Cody turned her pony loose to graze.

"Lucky horse," she exclaimed. "You won't go thirsty. There's a creek!" She took off her moccasins and waded into the water, drenching the hem of her skirt.

I took off my boots and socks, rolled up my leggings and splashed around with her. (Just because you're someone's guardian angel doesn't mean you can't paddle, right!)

Cody started collecting pebbles from the bottom of the creek. Among the tiny river stones she found an ancient arrowhead. I could feel that totally brought it home, that she was in a place that had been sacred to her father's people for like, *centuries*.

As the sun began to set, Cody found a patch of

ground under some scrubby little trees and arranged all her stones in a wide circle. Inside the circle she placed the few possessions she'd brought with her: her medicine bundle, the beaded pouch made by Jim Yellowbird's late wife, the photograph of her dad and one of Julia.

She quickly collected up a big pile of twigs and leaves, using her Navajo fire stick to kindle a fire as Butterfly Woman had shown her. Then she sat watching the leaping flames in the dusk, trying to ignore her growling belly.

Neither of us slept a wink that first night. Cody was too excited and I was on total red alert. Also the local wildlife gets v. v. active at nightfall! Huge moths kind of bumbled between my face and the stars, seeming as big as planets! Periodically I'd hear some unknown creature shriek or howl and hope it was just a coyote.

In the morning Cody woke to discover she'd camped over an ants' nest. I saw her staring around the canyon, eyes clouded with worry. I could hear what she was thinking. *What if the Holy People don't come*? She'd made this grand gesture, claiming her place in her father's tribe, not just as a "lost bird", but as Butterfly Woman's successor. If the Holy People didn't show up to support her, she'd for ever be the half-breed *chiindi* who went on a vision fast and came back with ants in her pants.

"Cody, those aren't your thoughts," I told her quietly.

Cody's eyes cleared like magic. She clenched her fists. "Can you hear me, Evil Ones?" she shouted into the canyon. "This time I'm not buying it! This time I decide when to leave!"

Leave, leave leave, mocked the echo.

She repacked her bag, moving her things to a hopefully ant-free spot. Later, scrambling about in the canyon, Cody found a feather, blue-black as her hair with a v. faint rainbow sheen. "I have no idea what bird that's from," she told Pepper. "I don't know the names of birds or which birds sing what songs. Owls go 'twit twoo', that's it! I live on this Earth and it's like I've been deaf and blind my whole life!"

"Oh, me too!" I said sympathetically. "Seagulls and pigeons, that's all I know."

"I never even went camping," Cody admitted.

"Nor me," I sighed. "Nowhere to plug in my hair straighteners."

"Too many bugs," shuddered Cody.

I knew we weren't really having a conversation, like Cody and Pepper weren't really having a conversation, but we both needed to feel like we were being heard.

At midday Cody climbed back up to the aunts'

camp, placed her first pebble by the door of their shelter, then hurried away. In the afternoon she ran about collecting plant material for her medicine bundle according to Butterfly Woman's instructions.

Out of respect for Cody's vision fast I'd left my trail mix behind and switched off my phone, but I couldn't resist snapping one little pic to show Lola. Crouching close to the red dirt of the canyon floor, examining dried seed pods, Cody was a different girl to the one the aunts rescued from the children's home. She even moved like a Navajo girl.

Later we set out to look for the cave, scrambling up the rocks, hunting for handholds. Cody found it by accident in the end. She slipped, quite badly, eventually hauling herself to safety using bits of old tree root to pull herself on to a stone ledge. There she found a keyhole-shaped opening just big enough to walk inside if we stooped.

As her eyes adjusted to the darkness inside, Cody gasped. The colours of the wall paintings were so fresh they could have been painted yesterday. Some of the subjects I recognised – a big buffalo hunt, Spider Woman weaving the Universe together with her sacred threads. Others showed Navajo mysteries too advanced for either me or Cody to decode.

Close by the entrance she found little kids' handprints.

Thousands of years old; they had literally become part of the rock. Cody tried to fit her hand over one of the prints. "I'm too big," she said wistfully.

That evening we had a singsong round the fire – my suggestion. "It's what kids do when they go camping," I told her. "Ten green bottles and whatever. I warn you though, I sound EXACTLY like a frog!"

As usual Cody picked up on my cue, but she had her own singsong ideas. She started singing, "Oh, you'll never get to Heaven on rollerskates, cos you'll roll right past those pearly gates!" Pepper made his way over, confused by all this unusual human-angel interaction.

"Mom and I used to sing that on long journeys when I was little," Cody told him. She stroked his nose lovingly. "I couldn't tell the aunts," she confessed, "but when I told Mom where I was, she completely freaked. I said, 'Mom, listen to what I'm telling you. I was in an institution, OK, and Dad's relatives came to take me home.' Mom said, 'But, honey, why didn't you stay with Elliot?' I said, 'He threw me out, Mom, remember? That's why I had to go in the home!' Then she cried. She said, 'The drugs make me muddle everything up. I'm a terrible mother, Cody, you should forget all about me.'" Cody covered her face and wept.

Next day, after she dropped off her pebble Cody came

back to camp and sat staring into space. I knew she was remembering her life with Julia.

The PODS can literally smell our hopelessness, panic or despair. Once they get a whiff, like bluebottles drawn to rotting meat, they come in crowds to feed. That night they were out there, I could feel it. So could Cody. The vision fast was peeling away all her normal defences, making her supersensitive to the Powers of Light and Darkness.

At 1:00 am she got up and put more wood on the fire, almost like she was warding off wolves, then huddled under her blanket, tensing at every sound. "It is a frightening thing to look into your own darkness," Butterfly Woman had warned. "Most people don't have the courage. Once you look, you are changed. Childhood is left behind for ever."

At 2:00 am Cody fell into an uneasy doze. At 2:45 am I could feel them closing in.

Oh, I knew they couldn't physically harm her. I had Cody's camp sealed with every protective symbol Mr Allbright had ever taught us. But as every angel child knows, the PODS prefer to destroy humans (and angels) from the *inside*.

At 3:00 am Cody began to toss and whimper in obvious distress.

"No, you don't," I muttered to the evil watchers.

"You're not pulling that old night terrors stunt, not on my beat you don't."

I'd been where Cody was now, remember? I'd come face to face with my own Darkness, though this was probably the first time I'd felt grateful for the experience. Thanks to The Test, I knew I had the strength to support Cody, to help her see this through. "Helix, crank up the vibes," I ordered. "I'm going in!"

I'm on it! she said calmly.

Bracing myself for just about anything, I beamed a tiny part of my energy into Cody's bad dream. I found her paralysed with terror in a creepy Hell dimension version of Rainbow Canyon. Nothing was right. Even Cody's circle of pebbles glowed with an icky, fungusy glow. Outside the circle something prowled. The creature went round and round and round in a way that made you want to scream. You could just hear its disgusting breathing.

I got mad then. So this was Cody's "curse". A piece of evil dream software, and it had kept her prisoner almost her whole life. I started talking to her in a firm, clear voice.

"I don't know if you can see me, but I'm right here with you, Cody, OK? I need you to do something really scary. I need you to tell this piece of cosmic slime to come out and show itself."

"I can't!" she gasped. "If a Skin Walker looks at you, you die!"

"No, no, it's just the opposite, sweetie. You'll start to live! It's like Butterfly Woman said. The Evil Ones put this nightmare into your head when you were a helpless little two-year-old, but you're not helpless now and you're not alone. We'll fight it together. Go on, tell it to show you what it's made of!"

Fists rigidly by her sides, Cody quavered, "Come out and show yourself."

"Do you want your life back or not?" I said sternly. "Then say it like you mean it! Say it like Butterfly Woman would say it."

Cody's expression changed. In a voice ringing with new authority, she shouted, "Come out and show yourself – NOW!"

Now now now, mocked the creepy dream echoes. There was a hideous roar and the creature came charging out of the darkness.

"Burning branch," I gabbled. "Right between the eyes. Do it now!" Cody grabbed a burning branch from the dream campfire and hurled it at the Skin Walker, which immediately, disgustingly exploded.

I gently extricated myself from Cody's dream to find her still clenching her fists. I listened to her peaceful breathing and shook my head. Smoke and mirrors.

Dark Studies 101. There never was a Skin Walker, just as Cody was never under a curse. It was always, always the PODS.

And we still had the fourth and final night to go.

CHAPTER TWENTY

When Cody came back from leaving her pebble next day, I could feel she was in a different place. She wrapped Butterfly Woman's blanket around her shoulders and sat peacefully gazing around the canyon. To me the rocks of Rainbow Canyon had always glowed with an inner light. This morning I knew Cody could see it too.

Standing up for herself in her dream had changed something for Cody. It wasn't important how the Skin Walker originally got a grip on her imagination. All that mattered was she had rooted the evil out for herself like Butterfly Woman said.

Cody's face was showing signs of her long fast, and there were dark shadows under her eyes, but her voice was strong as she began to chant the sacred words of the Blessing Way.

Beauty above me
Beauty below me
Beauty behind me
In beauty may I walk...

Nothing happened except it started to rain: fat, ice-cold drops that turned into a sudden mad downpour. There was an ugly ripping sound and livid blue and purple lightning forked down from the clouds.

Pepper's eyes rolled in terror. Suddenly he went galloping off, disappearing up the narrow cliff path, snorting and whinnying. Cody looked around her in alarm. She knew what Arizona lightning – plus cosmic spite – could do. The thought came to us at the same moment. The cave! Stuffing her blanket into her bag, Cody threw her possessions randomly on top and started to climb.

The soil was too dry. There was nothing to absorb the deluge. Cody slithered and slipped as water poured down the canyon face. A stab of lightning hit too close, making her lose her grip. She managed to save herself, just, but she hadn't had time to fasten her bag, and her belongings went spilling down into the canyon.

Cody made a frantic lunge, just managing to save her medicine bundle and her blanket, but the fire stick and the pictures were gone. Blinking water out of her eyes, Cody had no choice: she had to keep climbing as lightning struck the canyon over and over. Pink, green, yellow, blue, the flashes were every colour imaginable.

I'd known we'd have to face the Dark Side, but I never thought of Cody falling to her death, or being blasted with lightning. It felt almost like the Earth itself was out for revenge, zapping her with every weapon at its disposal. "Take that, human child!" Cody had stepped out of the dark circle, she'd defied the curse, but the curse was fighting back.

We reached the cave absolutely soaked. Cody wrung the rainwater out of her skirt, then sat shivering as the rain thundered past the cave mouth like a waterfall. The climb had used her last ounce of strength. She looked utterly defeated. "They didn't come," she whispered. "The Holy People didn't come."

"Get up!" I shouted. "You'll get pneumonia. Move your body."

Cody didn't move.

"I mean it! Don't sit there like a loser! You've got to give the Holy People something to work with, show them who they're dealing with!" I hardly knew what I was saying. I just knew Cody mustn't give up.

"Get up!" I repeated angrily. "Move your body. Dance!" I got it into my head that as her guardian angel I should take the lead, so I started to dance! Since you can't dance without music, I was pretty much forced to sing. (Me! Melanie the cartoon frog!) I sang the only song that popped into my head.

Born from the same star, you've come so far,
Born from the same star, you've come so far,
Earth's heart was aching, creation was
shattering and shaking...

I was singing Reuben's "Earth Song", only something strange was happening. As I sang, the original despairing lyrics somehow changed to words of hope:
But now you're waking, a new dawn is breaking...
It was like Reuben was right with me there in the cave, joining his voice with mine. Cody suddenly jumped up. With lightning bolts bouncing off the rocks like bursting bullets, she started to dance.

I never saw anyone dance the way Cody danced in that cave. It's like the storm was dancing *through* her, like she was literally playing with the same cosmic energies that had tried to destroy her.

Now they'll come, I thought excitedly. *Now it's going to happen.*

It did. With zigzags of pink and gold light whizzing and fizzing all around us, a voice spoke in the darkness of the cave.

"You are Cody Light-Dancing. That is your true Navajo name!"

The clear ringing female voice sounded strangely familiar. That's because it was MY voice!

The instant I spoke Cody's Navajo name the storm just stopped. Everything went utterly calm, like a more intense version of the dawn stillness I'd felt coming from Butterfly Woman.

Before I knew what was happening, the invisible barrier between the divine and human worlds dissolved and Cody and I were brought unexpectedly face to face.

"It's YOU!" she breathed. "You're the girl with butterfly boots. You were in my dream." Cody looked dazzled, shielding her eyes from the super-bright light that surrounded me. "Are you going to show me my life path?" she asked, trembling. "Is that why the Holy People sent you?"

I tried desperately not to look as confused as I felt. "Helix!" I said in a panic. "What do I say?" I knew that any words Cody heard now would influence her for the rest of her life.

Wing it, hon, Helix said serenely. *Just be yourself.*

At that exact moment just being myself didn't feel

like nearly enough. However, since the Universe had put me in the hotseat, I had to try to live up to it. So I opened my mouth, wondering with extreme interest what would come out.

I felt a sighing, golden breath on my face. Magically the words came one after another, like small perfect beads threading themselves on to a string, each one shimmering with divine energy.

"Your job is to help save the world, Cody! The twenty-first century is make or break time for humankind, and unless you do what you came to Earth to do, humans might not make it." Then I touched Cody's forehead, showing her the future that Ambriel and the other Creation angels had dreamed for her. They were totally using me as a channel by this time, so I got to see her vision at the same time she did.

The visions that come during a vision fast are v. sacred, not really to be spoken about. They also go on for HOURS. I'll just tell you that I saw Cody completing her training with Butterfly Woman, and going to college with Vickie and other bright, feisty Navajo girls. I also saw her travelling to different countries when she was still just a teenager, speaking out at conferences, telling governments they must listen to tribal peoples all over the world because they held the key to saving the planet. They always understood that the Earth and all its creatures never belonged to humans. It has always been the other way round...

When the visions finally stopped coming, Cody shakily opened her medicine bundle. She took out a nugget of raw crystal and left it on a ledge as a thank you to the Holy People for granting her a vision.

The invisible veil between the worlds had shimmered back into place, so Cody didn't see me unstring my favourite charm from the bracelet Reuben gave me for my birthday and place it carefully beside the crystal.

I followed Cody out into the silvery light of dawn and was shocked to realise we'd been in the cave all night. Slowly and carefully, because the rocks were still running with water and Cody was weak from hunger, the human girl and her guardian angel scrambled to the top of the canyon, where the aunts and the horses were all waiting.

Chapter Twenty-one

It turns out that being used as a channel by the Angels of Creation has v. interesting side-effects! I was still flying with the Creation vibes as we rode back to Ghost Canyon. Random scenes flashed through my mind: the moment in the cave when I heard Reuben singing with me, clear as day; Lola's story of the hunter who received a warning from a mysterious sorcerer with yellow eyes; singing the revised lyrics to Reuben's song, changes he couldn't possibly have made, unless, unless—

My heart started to thump so hard I couldn't breathe. Creation angels, Holy People, sorcerers: was it possible they were all just different names for the exact same divine beings? Names that varied according to time period or the beliefs of the locals? If so, I just might know what had happened to Reuben!

When we were in India, I'd learned that my planet had all kinds of secret cosmic access routes and short cuts, originally installed for the convenience of Creation angels when the Earth was new. Was it too huge a leap to wonder if they kept the odd secret bolt-hole for emergencies? The kind of cosmic space that doesn't necessarily show up on the Agency's radar? A space where a billion-year-old angel might take a family of endangered snow leopards – and the angel boy who'd been watching over them – to keep them safe from the Powers of Darkness?

By this time I was trembling so hard it took three goes to switch on my mobile. Before I could hit speed dial, my phone burst into the opening bars of our cosmic theme tune.

"*Carita*, he's here! He just walked into the hut. Mel, can you hear me? Mel?"

Back in Ghost Canyon Cody fell into bed and slept for eighteen hours straight. Then she got up and ate such an enormous plate of stew the aunts could only watch in awe.

Aunt Bonita waited till her niece finished eating then lit a cigarette. Cody gently removed it from her fingers.

Ignoring her aunts' shocked exclamations, she stubbed it out on her plate.

"I need you to still be here for a long time," she told them with a sad little smile. "I need you to all be alive and quarrelling when I come back to the Navajo nation."

"*Come back!*" said the aunts with one voice. "You're leaving?"

I felt like I'd been slapped. How could she leave now, after what she'd seen in the cave! What about her apprenticeship with Butterfly Woman? What happened to saving the world?

"I can't live on the reservation," Cody explained. "It's too far from Mom. She hasn't got anyone apart from me. It'll mean me going into care, but I can handle that. I'll come back in the holidays, if that's OK? I couldn't not come back, not now."

Aunt Bonita distractedly picked up her cigarettes, then dropped them as if she'd scorched her fingers. "There's another possibility," she said very quietly. "We all drive on up to Maryland, spring your mom outa the hospital, and bring her back to live here?"

Cody's eyes slowly filled with tears. "Why would you do that? My mom's really sick. She's been sick her whole life."

"The Navajo got people like that too," Aunt Jeannie

put in gently. "We just have our own ways of looking after them."

"But she's not even Navajo!" Cody was openly weeping now.

"Pouf, old-time Navajo people used to do that all the time," Aunt Bonita said nonchalantly. "They were constantly taking white people hostage. By the time the cavalry showed up the hostages were having so much fun, they just refused to be rescued! That's why so many Navajo got foreign names. White, Latino, African American, we're the original rainbow tribe!"

I could feel shaky excitement in Cody. Was it truly possible? Could she really live her dream AND take care of Julia?

"We'll fetch your mama back in time for the dance," said Aunt Evalina, as if it was all decided.

"There's going to be a dance?" said Cody.

"The biggest in living memory," said Aunt Bonita.

Angels get a particular feeling when it's time to leave Earth. It's like a shimmery musical note no one else can hear.

I blew them a kiss, then tiptoeing out of the trailer I settled myself on the rusty swing. Through the open window I could hear Cody and her aunts excitedly making plans. Closing my eyes in the Arizona sunlight, I waited for the Agency to beam me back home.

Chapter Twenty-two

Sometimes the Universe sends all our Christmases at once.

I'd just cleared Arrivals, and I was literally on my phone calling Lola to find out when they were due back, when I saw her and Brice in cold-weather gear firmly marching in my direction at the head of a crowd of angel trainees. They all looked v. v. focused like they were still on a mission.

They got to a few metres away from me, then the sea of trainees suddenly parted to let someone through. It was Reuben, tired, smiling, totally unharmed. I just stood like a dummy until he was right beside me.

"Did you get my text about Millie?" Reubs deliberately

spoke too quietly for anyone else to hear. I nodded, silently drinking him in. "So what do you think?"

"I – I was actually a bit confused," I fibbed. "What are you saying exactly? That there's like a cosmic vacancy?" (Well, no one respects a pushover, do they?)

Reuben shook his head. "No vacancy. There's only one angel girl for me. If I can't have her, I don't want anyone."

He looked so totally desperate that having held out for all of two seconds I just walked into his arms – to loud cheers and wolf whistles from the watching trainees.

Somewhere Lola was shrieking, "Oh that's SO SWEET!"

"Ahh! Finally brought together by the PODS!" Brice mocked.

But I was deaf and blind to everything else. My beautiful angel boy was safely home at last.

Next day I was called to Michael's office, where he told me I'd been put in for a special HALO award. He said Ambriel could only use me as a channel for the Creation angels visions because I was so totally in tune with Cody. The old-style Navajo approach wouldn't have worked with her at ALL.

He said some v. flattering things which I don't want to repeat because that would make me sound

SERIOUSLY grandiose! Then as I was leaving he said calmly, "Obviously, you're going to the dance?"

Everyone came as it turned out! Angel kids from my school, trainees who'd read about Cody in the blog I started after I got back to Heaven, including Earth angels I'd worked with on missions. Michael came with super high-ups from the Agency. Apparently Cody was the best news the Agency had had in a v. long time. As for Ambriel and his friends – well, you can imagine why they wanted to be there.

The night was in full swing by the time we arrived. Like most big Navajo celebrations this was being held in the open air. Every time the musicians took a break, teenagers with twig brooms ran on to sweep the trodden earth, spraying water to keep down the dust.

"Can you see her?" Lola kept saying. "Can you see Cody?"

I quickly spotted Vickie and Earl. I saw Julia chatting to Lily Topaha. I saw Roxie, Dwayne, Tazbah and the new baby.

Lola pulled my sleeve, "Isn't that her? Wow! Cody lucked out when she got you as her guardian angel. A new name, a new life and angelic style tips thrown in!"

I shook my head in wonder. I'd been looking for a girl in grey! But this calm, smiling Cody was wearing the exact vibey colours I wore on my mission!"

Several Navajo musicians in traditional tribal clothes walked on to the makeshift stage, carrying a set of massive log-shaped drums. "This should be worth hearing!" Reubs said in my ear.

The drummers started pounding out a beat you could literally feel thudding in the roots of your teeth. All the Navajo elders launched into some kind of stomping circle dance, and the younger Navajo gradually joined in. They did it like they were humouring the oldies, but really it was the wild rhythms pulling them into the dance. I saw Jim Yellowbird catch hold of a surprised-looking Julia, dragging her into the circle.

Ambriel was watching from the far side of the circle. He gave me the thumbs up that had become our little joke. I waved happily and felt Reuben's hand reach for mine in the dark. "You can stop bugging everyone now," he teased softly. "You finally found out why they made you an angel."

It turns out that my life has been influenced by Cody Fortuna just as much as hers has been influenced by her guardian angel. Seeing her wake up and start to live Ambriel's dream had set me buzzing with excitement and hope! Actually it set me wondering. Maybe more kids in my century could wake up and remember who they really were. Maybe, like Cody, they just needed the right kind of cosmic support. Then the Agency's plans for Earth could go ahead like they were supposed to.

I kicked these thoughts around with Reuben, and after a LOT of late-night talks, we came up with this super-wild idea. Our friends and teachers came on board and the whole thing went supernova!

From next week our cosmic roadshow is going to be hitting the streets of the twenty-first century, hunting out gifted kids like Cody before the Dark Agencies get to them.

Remember that spine-tingling moment when your misty prehistoric planet burst into flower? This is like that moment, only this time it's humans who get to make that impossible leap to the next level!

For now, though, just picture me and Reubs grooving to the Navajo beat, until Lola and Brice grab our hands and we find ourselves being pulled into the madly spinning stomping dance, whirling our way into the most thrilling part of the story where angels and humans finally join together to heal the Earth.

*Read Mel's angelic adventures
from the very beginning...*

winging it

TIME: My 13th Birthday

PLACE: Heaven

MISSION: Enrol at angel school!

REPORT: One minute I'm crossing the road then – BANG! – I'm a student at angel school, learning about halos. At least the uniforms are cool...

losing the plot

TIME: 16th Century

PLACE: London

MISSION: Rescue a teenage trio!

REPORT: A "delicate situation" our Archangel calls it. Chaos more like! The PODS are strong, that creepy agent Brice is in town and we have to act fast...

flying high

TIME: 13th Century

PLACE: France

MISSION: Prepare to party!

REPORT: We're heading to France for a Children's Crusade. But there's an evil time-travel scam going on – and I'm still wearing my silk sarong and flip-flops!

calling the shots

TIME: 20th Century

PLACE: Hollywood

MISSION: Get into showbiz!

REPORT: My first mission as a solo Guardian Angel and I've got serious stage fright! It may look angelic in the movies, but life is dangerous in Tinsel Town…

fogging over

TIME: 19th Century

PLACE: Australia and London

MISSION: Take a trip down under!

REPORT: I get to choose our next assignment. But why Australia when I asked for London? And what is my soul-mate Lola doing holding hands with bad boy Brice?

fighting fit

TIME: 1st Century AD

PLACE: Rome

MISSION: Get into the gladiator groove!

REPORT: The boy of my dreams, Orlando, wants a team of angel volunteers to go to Ancient Rome, so guess who's first in the queue...

making waves

TIME: 17th Century

PLACE: Jamaica

MISSION: Foil the pirates!

REPORT: When our teacher tells us we're going to the Caribbean, I'm like, "Woo, I am SO packing my bikini!" I just wish I'd listened to the bit about pirates...

budding star

TIME: 21st Century

PLACE: Japan

MISSION: Rescue a pop princess!

REPORT: Chasing the soul of a Japanese pop star is a new one for me! Castles, ninjas and magicians aside, someone is playing a dark game, and I think I know who...